W9-BYZ-202

Death *of a* Policeman

Previous Hamish Macbeth Mysteries by M. C. Beaton

M. C. BEATON

Death *of a* Policeman

GRAND CENTRAL
PUBLISHING

NEW YORK   BOSTON

Grand Central Publishing
Hachette Book Group
237 Park Avenue
New York, NY 10017

www.HachetteBookGroup.com

Printed in the United States of America

RRD-C

First Edition: February 2014
10 9 8 7 6 5 4 3 2 1

Grand Central Publishing is a division of Hachette Book Group, Inc.
The Grand Central Publishing name and logo is a trademark of Hachette Book Group, Inc.

The Hachette Speakers Bureau provides a wide range of authors for speaking events. To find out more, go to www.hachettespeakersbureau.com or call (866) 376-6591.

The publisher is not responsible for websites (or their content) that are not owned by the publisher.

Library of Congress Cataloging-in-Publication Data

Beaton, M. C.
  Death of a policeman / M. C. Beaton. — First Edition.
     pages cm
  ISBN 978-1-4555-0473-2 (hardback) — ISBN 978-1-4555-7625-8 (large print hardcover) — ISBN 978-1-4789-2544-6 (audio download)
  1. Police—Fiction. 2. Murder—Investigation—Fiction. 3. Scotland—Fiction. I. Title.
  PR6053.H4535D34 2014
  823'.914—dc23
                              2013018529

To David and Janis Weir
with affection

Death *of a* Policeman

Chapter One

☠

A watched pot never boils.
　　　　　　—proverb, mid nineteenth century

The fact that all the police forces in Scotland were to be amalgamated into one large force struck terror into police headquarters in Strathbane. It was said that all over Scotland three thousand auxiliary jobs would be lost, which would mean more work for the actual police themselves. Then would they start chopping heads of the very police force itself.

Only one man was happy at the news—Detective Chief Inspector Blair. Surely this might be the opportunity to get rid of Police Sergeant Hamish Macbeth and winkle him out of his cosy station in Lochdubh. He could not understand how Hamish had been able to hang on with local police stations closing down all over Scotland.

But he experienced a setback when he broached the idea

to his chief, Superintendent Daviot. "Sutherland is a huge county," said Daviot, "and it is surely economical to have Macbeth cover all of it."

"But most of the time, he and his sidekick, Fraser, just mooch around doing nothing," complained Blair.

"We have no proof of that," said Daviot severely. "You should be worried about your own job."

"Whit!"

"I am sure we will have officials soon crawling all over us to see what they can cut," said Daviot.

Blair took himself off to the pub to crouch over a double whisky and try to work out a plan. If he could prove that Hamish Macbeth did little, then he could send in a report to the new authorities. But who would be low enough to spy on Macbeth?

After another double whisky, his brain seemed to clear. Cyril Sessions was a fairly new constable, nicknamed Romeo because of his good looks. Shortly after his arrival from Perth, Blair had uncovered evidence that Cyril had been enjoying the favours of a prostitute, without paying her a penny. She had finally cracked and reported Cyril. Blair got the complaint and confronted Cyril. Cyril had pleaded and begged and said he would do anything if Blair made the complaint go away.

Cunningly, Blair decided to keep this ally in the bank, so to speak, until such time as he would need to draw on him. He phoned headquarters and asked Cyril to join him.

Women in the pub stared appreciatively at Cyril when

he entered. He was of medium height with glossy black hair, blue eyes in a square handsome face, and a muscular figure.

"Sit down, my lad," said Blair. "I've a wee job for you. I want evidence that Hamish Macbeth in Lochdubh does bugger-all when it comes to policing."

"Isn't that the man who's got a grand reputation for solving murders?"

"I was me that solved them," said Blair, "while that slimy toad took the credit. You owe me a favour, or do I need to remind you that I had to threaten that brass nail to keep her painted mouth shut?"

"Brass nail?"

"Where have you been? Brass nail. Screw. Get it? That prossy you were banging."

"Oh, aye. That."

"Aye, that. Here's what you've got tae do. Take a fishing holiday in Lochdubh and get photos of Macbeth lounging around. His policeman, Dick Fraser, often sleeps in a deck chair in the front garden. Get a good shot o' that. Macbeth doesn't know you, so you can get real close. Chat with the locals. Pick up gossip."

"I don't fish."

"Well, rambling or something like that. The Highlands are fu' o' hairy-legged bastards farting ower the hills."

"When do I start?"

"Soon as you can. I want this done and dusted before numpties from the new police arrangement descend on us."

Cyril looked at him shrewdly. "Have you tried this before?"

Blair shifted his fat haunches on the bar stool. He had, in fact, and it had ended with his spy nearly getting killed. But he had no intention of telling Cyril anything about it.

"No, just thought o' it," he said. "Get moving and fix that holiday."

Hamish was actually working at that moment. Lairg sheep sales are the biggest in Europe, and he was policing them with Dick at his side. Because of the size of the sales, Strathbane had sent up two policemen to assist him. The importance of the yearly event meant that crofters were often dressed in the sort of finery people thought were the reserve of tourists: deerstalkers, tall crooks, kilts and sporrans.

Hamish and Dick strolled into the beer tent late in the day and found their other two colleagues. "Everyone upset about the new Scottish police force?" asked Hamish, joining them.

"You can say that again," said one of them. "Take off the civilian staff, and think o' the extra paperwork."

"And how's my dear friend, Blair?" asked Hamish.

The other policeman sniggered, "I think he's in lurv."

"Who's the lucky lady?"

"It's a bloke. Fairly new copper called Cyril Sessions. Real handsome chap. Blair's been seen drinking with him all over the place. Can't get enough of his company."

* * *

As they walked out of the beer tent, Dick said sententiously, "It does happen, you know."

"What does?" asked Hamish.

"Fellows when they get on a bit. They wake up to the fact that they prefer other blokes to their missus."

"Oh, aye? Well, the only love affair Blair's ever had is with the booze. He's plotting something."

"Do you mind if I hurry off?" said Dick anxiously. "I'm due down in Strathbane."

"Another quiz?"

"Aye, and the prize is a brand-new Volvo."

"Off you go. Things are quiet here."

Hamish switched on the television that evening. Dick had such a reputation for winning quiz competitions that Hamish was surprised they let him on.

The questions seemed to be very difficult. Six contestants were quickly whittled down to two, Dick and a shabby old man. And then Dick lost at the last question: how long does it take light from the moon to reach the earth?

The old man said quickly, "One point two six seconds." There was a roll of drums and cheers from the audience as he was led to the gleaming new car.

Hamish waited up until a weary Dick arrived home. "Not like you to lose," said Hamish. "That must be the first time."

"I couldnae do it to him," said Dick.

"What?"

"He was an auld crofter. He'd never been on one of thae quiz shows before. The stories o' hardship he told me in the green room. It would ha' been wicked not to let the poor auld soul win."

"What was his name again?"

"Henry McQueen. Got a bittie o' a place outside Bonar Bridge."

"I wonder if there's anything on the computer about him," said Hamish.

"Why?"

"Just a hunch. I've got a feeling I saw him at the sheep sales."

Dick followed Hamish into the police office. Hamish switched on the computer and searched for Henry McQueen's name. "There's something here from last year's *Highland Times*," said Hamish, clicking it open. "There you are. I thought I'd heard of him. He took top price for his lambs two years' running. You were conned. Oh, here's another link. Five years ago he came out top on *Mastermind*. Subject. The Epistles of St. Paul."

"I'll murder the auld creep," raged Dick.

"Oh, leave it. I'm sure he'll crop up again," said Hamish soothingly, "and then you can wipe the floor with him."

The following day, Cyril checked into Mrs. Mackenzie's bed-and-breakfast on the waterfront at Lochdubh. He dumped his haversack in a small room and wondered how long he could put up with pretending to be a rambler, particularly as he had arrived in his car. He had pointed out to Blair that he was surely not going to be able to follow Macbeth around on foot.

The room was at the back of the house. It was cold. There was a meter on the wall with a sign that pound coins had to be deposited for electricity. The bed was narrow and covered in rough blankets under a pink candlewick spread. A print of Jesus feeding the multitude with loaves and fishes hung over the blocked-up fireplace. Underneath was the legend, HIS EYE IS ON THE SPARROW. On a rickety table by the bed was a large Bible. The room was fairly dark. Cyril popped a coin in the meter and switched on the light in a glass bowl above his head full of dead flies. He hung his clothes in the curtained alcove which served as a wardrobe. There was neither a phone nor a television set. The only reason, he thought, that she got any customers was because Mrs. Mackenzie charged cheap rates.

He decided to go out for a walk around the village and start work.

The day outside was warmer than his room. A pale October sun shone down on a row of whitewashed cottages, fronting the sea loch. It looked like a picture postcard. Cyril walked towards the harbour. He brightened when he saw a pub. He would start with a drink and see what he could find out from the locals. There was a silence when he entered. He ordered a vodka and tonic.

A small man in tight clothes materialised at his elbow and said, "Are you on holiday?"

"Yes," said Cyril. "I'm Jamie Mackay up from Perth."

"Archie Maclean," said the little man.

"Let me buy you a drink," said Cyril, "and maybe we could sit over at that table by the window. I'd like to get to know a bit about the village."

Archie ordered a double whisky. Cyril realised that Blair had said nothing about paying for his work. Conversation rose again as they made their way to the table.

"So what are you doing here?" asked Archie.

"I came up by car, but I might do a bit of walking."

Archie's sharp blue eyes in his nut-brown face dropped to look at Cyril's highly polished black shoes. "I hope you've got boots with you," he said. "You won't get far in those."

"Yes, I've got boots," said Cyril. He wondered why the little man wore such tight clothes, not knowing that Archie's wife washed all his clothes so that they shrank.

"So, much crime around here?" asked Cyril.

"No, it's fair quiet."

"I saw a police station. Not much for a copper to do up here."

"Hamish Macbeth, the police sergeant, covers a big part o' Sutherland," said Archie. "He's got a lot tae do. Thanks for the drink, laddie. Got tae go."

Hamish was seated at the kitchen table when Archie burst through the door. "What's up?" asked Hamish.

"'Member the time when that scunner Blair put a copper on yer tail to report on ye?"

"As if it were yesterday," said Hamish. "Has he sent another?"

"Could be," said Archie, sitting down at the table. "Could I hae wan o' your espresso coffees? The wifie doesnae hold wi' coffee."

"That's Dick's machine. I don't know how to operate it. I'll fetch him. He's sleeping in the garden."

Hamish strolled round to the front of the police station just in time to see the figure of Cyril snapping a photograph of Dick asleep in his deck chair. He nipped round onto the road and confronted Cyril. "What's so special about a photograph of a man in a deck chair?" asked Hamish.

"I'm a bit of an amateur photographer," said Cyril. "I thought I'd enter it for a competition and call it *Sleeping Policeman*."

"Visiting?"

"Yes. Good place for walks."

"Where are you staying?" asked Hamish.

"Mrs. Mackenzie's. I'll be getting along."

Cyril strode off. Hamish stared after him. Then he went into the office and phoned Detective Jimmy Anderson.

"How are things up in peasantville?" asked Jimmy.

"Weird."

"It's aye weird up there."

"There's this fellow turned up and took a photo of Dick asleep in the garden. Handsome chap with black curly hair, tall, blue eyes, little half-moon scar above the right eye, but with policeman's shoes on and black socks. Says he's going to be going for walks. Anyone missing from headquarters who looks like that?"

"There's one smarmy bastard who sucks up to Blair. Cyril Sessions."

"I knew it!" exclaimed Hamish. "Blair is out to get proof that there's no crime up here. I'll get that photo back somehow."

Hamish woke Dick up and explained the situation. He ended by saying, "Let's see if we can lose the cheil for an hour. Give Archie a mug o' espresso first."

They walked over to the harbour fifteen minutes later, where Archie Maclean was sitting on a bollard, rolling a cigarette. "No tourists today?" asked Hamish. Fishing stocks were dwindling, and so Archie supplemented his income by taking tourists on trips round the loch.

"I've only got a couple. They'll be along in a minute."

"Do me a favour. Yon chap you met in the pub is one o' Blair's snoops. He'll be hanging around. He's staying at Mrs. Mackenzie's. Offer him a free trip in your boat."

"Aye, right. Want me to tip him ower the side?"

"No, just keep him away. If he's got his camera with him, try to stage an accident to it that makes it look as if it's his fault."

Archie scurried off. He found Cyril outside Mrs. Mackenzie's. Cyril was delighted to accept. It would be a chance to find out more about Macbeth.

Hamish stood at his living room window, watching, until

he saw the fishing boat sail out into the loch. Then he hurried along to Mrs. Mackenzie's bed-and-breakfast.

Before he got there, he met the Currie sisters, twins Nessie and Jessie, on the waterfront. They were very alike. Although the day was sunny, there was a nip in the air, and so they had reverted to their winter wear of camel-hair coats, headscarves, and brogues.

"Grand day," said Hamish. "Have you seen the newcomer?"

"We have that," said Nessie. "Like a fillum star."

"Fillum star," echoed the Greek chorus that was Jessie.

"It's refreshing to find a young man who kens so much about the Bible," said Hamish. "He's out with Archie, but when he gets back, you should invite him to tea. Right religious, he is."

"We'll do that," said Nessie. "It will be nice to talk to a clean young man instead o' a lazy philanderer like yourself."

"Like yourself," came her sister's echo.

Hamish walked on and knocked at the door of the bed-and-breakfast. Mrs. Mackenzie was a small woman, wearing a flower-patterned overall and with her hair tied up in a headscarf. The lines on her face were permanently set in disapproval.

"Whit?" she demanded.

"I would like a look at the newcomer's room," said Hamish. "We've had a tip-off."

"Then he can pack his bags and get out."

"No, no," said Hamish soothingly. "Don't tell him I

called. Chust a routine enquiry. You don't want to go losing a paying customer at this time of year. Chust a wee peek in his room."

"Oh, all right. Top o' the stairs on the left. The door is-nae locked. I was up there cleaning."

Hamish nipped up the stairs and into Cyril's room. There was a computer lying on the bed, but what he wanted was the camera. There was no sign of it. He could only hope that Archie would find a way to get rid of it.

Archie let his mate, Ally Harris, take wheel while he pointed out various landmarks to the two tourists, a husband and wife, and Cyril. Cyril was standing at the side of the boat, his camera slung round his neck.

Moving behind him, Archie took out a sharp knife and sliced almost through the strap at the back of Cyril's neck.

He said, "If youse will look ower the side, that's where the kelpie is supposed tae live."

"What's a kelpie?" asked the female.

"It's a creature that appears as a sea horse and sometimes changes into a beautiful wumman," said Archie. "It goes af-ter wee bairns. It gets them to stroke it and it's adhesive and when they stick to it, it drags them down into the loch and eats them. It's supposed to live right down there. Lean right ower and you'll maybe see it."

Cyril and the tourists leaned over. "There is something down there," said Cyril excitedly. A black shape could be seen moving in the murky depths. His camera was swinging from his neck by the strap. Just as he was reaching for it, the strap broke and his camera dropped down into the water.

A seal surfaced and stared up at them as Cyril let out a wail of dismay.

"You should ha' got yourself wan o' thae wee yins you can carry in your pocket," said Archie. "I hivnae seen wan like that in years. If you go to Patel's shop, you can buy wan o' thae cheap throwaway ones."

"It was a friend's camera," said Cyril. He cursed Blair, who had given him an old Rolleiflex camera out of storage at headquarters, saying it was better than any newfangled one. He did have a Canon pocket one inside his jacket. At least he would be more comfortable using that.

Archie telephoned Hamish to say that Cyril's camera was now somewhere at the bottom of the loch, and Hamish heaved a sigh of relief.

Before, when he had been under threat, he had manufactured a crime wave with the help of the locals. But Hamish was feeling lazy, enjoying the rare good weather of the autumn.

Cyril had read up on Hamish's successful cases and knew that several had taken place in the town of Braikie. The following day, he decided to visit the town, hoping the residents there might have less favourable ideas about Hamish than the villagers. He had gone to the village stores and after leaning on the counter, talking about the weather, he asked the owner, Mr. Patel, what he thought of the local policeman. Mr. Patel had smiled and launched on a paean of praise about Hamish.

Cyril had then gone to the Italian restaurant for dinner and quizzed the waiter, Willie Lamont. His heart sank when it turned out that Hamish was godfather to Willie's child. Was no one going to criticise the man?

But in Braikie, his hopes sank lower. The people he talked to did not know Hamish personally but knew his reputation for solving murders and seemed to be proud to have such a policeman looking after them.

He was passing the library when he noticed they had a sign outside saying there were books for sale. Cyril decided to buy some light reading and walked into the Victorian gloom of the building.

Hetty Dunstable, the librarian, saw a handsome man looking around and teetered forward on her high heels. "Can I help you?"

Cyril saw a small, thin woman in her early forties wearing a near-transparent white blouse over a tight skirt. She had a small, pinched face and bulging brown eyes. Cyril thought sourly that she looked like a rabbit with myxomatosis. But he gave his most charming smile and said, "I saw that you had books for sale."

"Yes, they're over here," said Hetty, leading the way to a wooden bench. "These are the ones that are too damaged to remain on the shelves. Are you new to the area?"

"Just on holiday," said Cyril. "I'm over in Lochdubh."

"Keep clear of the police station. Hamish Macbeth is useless."

"I'd like to hear more," said Cyril. "I enjoy a bit of gossip with a pretty girl. When do you get off?"

"We close up in ten minutes."

"Let's go for a drink."

"Yes, I would love that," said Hetty.

Hetty had no intention of telling this gorgeous man her real reason for disliking Hamish. She had once invited Hamish to a party at her flat after having met him on one of his investigations. Hamish was not interested. But she had drunk too much and had thrown herself at him, calling him her darling. Hamish had gently pushed her away and gone home. Her friends teased her about it until she began to think Hamish had wronged her. She told them so many times that Hamish had led her on that she began to believe it.

Cyril was often seen in Hetty's company in the following days. Then to Hetty's dismay, he said he would be too busy to see her. Hetty began to feel guilty. She was sure Cyril was spying on Hamish and wondered if he was a villain. She had made up a lot of malicious stories about Hamish's laziness. If anything happened to Hamish, the investigation would lead back to her.

She at last phoned Hamish and said someone called Jamie Mackay had been asking a lot of questions about him.

"Don't worry," said Hamish. "I know all about him," correctly guessing that Jamie was Cyril.

"What will you do?" asked Hetty.

"Take my shotgun and blow the bugger's head off," said Hamish and rang off.

"Let's give Cyril something to do tomorrow," Hamish said to Dick. "We'll race off tomorrow up north and give the lad something to chase. The beasties are getting fat. They need some exercise."

Hamish's "beasties" consisted of a wild cat called Sonsie and a dog called Lugs. "I'll get a picnic ready," said Dick.

Hamish felt a stab of irritation. He wished Dick would not be so—well—*domesticated*. He felt Dick had taken the place of a possible wife, and Hamish often dreamt of marriage. His love affair with television presenter Elspeth Grant had recently fallen through. He had once been engaged to Priscilla Halburton-Smythe, daughter of the retired colonel who owned the Tommel Castle Hotel, but it just hadn't worked out.

At that moment, Cyril was ensconced in the Currie sisters' parlour, balancing a cup of tea on one knee. He had hoped the sisters would give him some gossip about Hamish, but they seemed hell-bent on quizzing him about the King James version of the Bible.

"Beautiful words," said Nessie. "'I am the voice of one, crying in the wilderness.'"

"I couldn't agree more," said Cyril, ignoring Jessie's echo. He thought, if I don't get out of this damn place soon I'll go mad. "You were saying something about the local policeman."

"No, I wasn't," said Nessie.

"Bit of a layabout, is he?"

"We do not gossip in this village," said Nessie righteously. "Pass me the Bible, Jessie, and we'll hear this nice young man read to us."

It was a large Victorian Bible, illustrated with steel engravings. Feeling trapped, Cyril began to read, and, as he read, he began to experience a strange feeling of doom. His mobile phone suddenly rang and he grabbed it out of his pocket. It was Blair, asking if there was any progress.

"Can't talk now, Mother," said Cyril. "I'll call you later." He rang off.

"You shouldn't cut your mother off like that," chided Nessie.

"How right you are." Cyril stood up and put the Bible and his cup on the table. "I'll get back to my digs and call her from there."

"We'll see you in the kirk on Sunday," said Nessie.

If I'm still alive and not dead with boredom, thought Cyril, making his escape.

"Where are we off to?" asked Dick the next morning as he climbed into the Land Rover beside Hamish.

"Do you know Sandybeach?"

"No, where's that?"

"Tiny little place up north of Scourie. Grand place for a picnic. I'll put the siren on and get Cyril chasing us."

"It's only seven in the morning," said Dick. "Think he'll be up yet?"

"Probably not. But I've phoned Jimmy. Blair's bound to ask if there's been a report of a crime so I told him to say there was a burglary at Sandybeach."

"So what do we do if the scunner catches up with us?"

"He won't. It's so quiet up there, you can hear a car coming for miles. We'll take off for somewhere else."

The sound of the siren woke Cyril. He tumbled out of bed and dashed to the window, opened it and hung out. He could just see the Land Rover racing out over the hump-backed bridge. He scrabbled into his clothes and phoned Blair, asking him to find out where Hamish had gone.

He had gone a mile out of Lochdubh when Blair rang. "Burglary at a place called Sandybeach."

"Where's that?"

"How should I know? Look at a map."

Cyril programmed his sat-nav and set off in pursuit. He hurtled along the one-track roads, blind to the beauty all around him. Purple heather blazed on the flanks of the soaring mountains. Rowan trees shone with blood-red berries. Above, the sky was an arch of blue. At one point, he thought he heard the sound of another driver behind him and suddenly stopped, switched off his engine, rolled down the windows, and listened. But there was nothing to be heard but the mournful call of a curlew.

Cyril crouched over the wheel and drove on.

Sutherland, the southland of the Vikings, is the most underpopulated county in the British Isles. The west coast has the most dazzling scenery. But to Cyril, it was an odd foreign landscape, alien, far from the bustle and crowds of Strathbane.

At long last, he saw a signpost pointing the way to Sandybeach.

"The end of the road," said Cyril, not knowing that, for him, it was.

Chapter Two

Good Lord, what is man! for as simple he looks,
Do but try to develop his hooks and his crooks,
With his depth and his shallows, his good and his evil,
All in all he's a problem must puzzle the devil.
— *Robert Burns*

"Aren't we going to Sandybeach?" asked Dick as Hamish drove past the turn.

"We'll go a bit further on. I don't want that man skulking around. There's a nice beach a bit along here. Blair's probably told him where we're heading. Let him have a useless day."

The police Land Rover bumped down a heathery track and onto a curve of white sand sheltered by tall cliffs. Hamish let his pets out, and Dick got busy spreading out the picnic.

Dick held up a chicken leg. "Try this. It's real free-range."

"Not one of mine, I hope," said Hamish, who preferred to let his hens die of old age.

"No. Chap ower at the forestry keeps grand birds."

They ate and drank contentedly, watching deep blue waves smash onto the beach. Seagulls screamed and dived overhead, creating a loud cacophony of sound.

Hamish eventually tipped his hat over his eyes and fell asleep.

After half an hour, he suddenly woke and sat up. "Pack up, Dick. We may as well head back. Cyril's probably given up by now."

They drove up out of the bay. Hamish suddenly stopped and lowered the window. "I thought I heard something." He could faintly hear a car horn in the distance. It seemed to be signalling SOS.

Earlier, Cyril had arrived at Sandybeach. He could only see the ruins of three buildings. How could anyone report a burglary when there was no one there? He had a creeping feeling that Hamish had deliberately led him on a wild goose chase and that Hamish knew exactly who he was. He took out his mobile to call Blair but found he could not get a signal.

He got out of his car and walked along the beach. The day was warm, and there was only the scream of the gulls and the crashing of giant waves on the beach.

Then he heard the sound of a vehicle approaching. It must be Macbeth, he thought. There was nothing he could do but brazen it out. He would say he had followed Hamish because he thought it would be exciting to witness a police investigation and hope Hamish believed him.

He relaxed when he saw a motorcyclist bumping down the tussocky path, the sun glinting on the rider's black helmet. Cyril decided to get back into his car and drive off.

He had just reached his car when he became aware of a presence behind him and swung round. The blast from a sawn-off shotgun took him full in the chest. Two seagulls at the water's edge rose screaming up to the sky, higher and higher, as if bearing off Cyril's soul.

The cyclist wheeled his bike back to the track. Then the cyclist returned with a brush and bent down and brushed away any footprints and tyre tracks before getting back on the bike and roaring off.

Silence fell on the beach again. Blood seeped from Cyril's chest wound to darken the white sand.

Ten minutes later, along the road above, came a sleek Mercedes. The driver was Terence Hardy, a builder's merchant from Essex with his wife, Kylie, and his teenage son, Wayne.

He braked above the beach and cried, "Look at that! You can get some swimming, Wayne."

"Don't want to swim," muttered his son, fiddling with his iPad.

"You'll swim if I say so," said his father. "I'll leave the car here and we'll walk down."

Kylie repressed a sigh. Why couldn't they have gone to

Marbella as usual? She could be lying by the pool with a cold drink instead of being stuck up here in this godforsaken part of the British Isles that none of her friends had heard of.

Wayne sprinted down the path to the beach. Maybe he might find a shop where he could buy a can of Red Bull.

He stopped short at the sight of Cyril. He looked wildly around to see if there were any cameras. He could hear his mother and father having a vicious fight. "I wanna go home," his mother was screaming.

"This is real beauty," shouted her husband. "You ought to be creaming your jeans. What…?"

He stared at his white-faced son.

"Dad, there's a dead man on the beach."

"Let me see. If you're lying, I'll take my belt to you."

Burly Terence in his gleaming white trainers, jeans with knife-edged pleats, and T-shirt with the legend ESSEX FOR SEX strode down to the beach.

He walked up to Cyril's body. His knees began to tremble. Terence stumbled back up to the car. "I'll get the police," he said. "He's murdered."

But he could not get a signal on his phone. His terrified wife began to scream like a banshee. In desperation, Terence began to honk out SOS on the car horn.

"Dad, let's get out of here!" shouted Wayne. "The murderer might still be around."

"Get in the car," roared Terence, turning as white as his son.

At that moment Hamish came roaring up in the Land Rover. He jumped down and caught Kylie as she threw herself into his arms, babbling about murder.

He gently put her aside. "Where's the body?" he asked Terence.

"On the beach."

"Wait here. Constable Fraser will take your statements."

Hamish ran down to the beach. He stood for a moment, looking sadly down at Cyril's dead body. He felt for a pulse in the faint hope there might be some life left, but there was none.

He tried his mobile phone without success. He went back to the Land Rover and got on the radio, summoning help.

Then he approached the Hardy family. "I'm afraid you will need to wait a bit. Detectives and forensics will be here soon."

"I have their statements," said Dick. "They're staying at the Tommel Castle Hotel."

"I'll need to change," said Kylie. "I peed myself."

"You can use the back of the police Land Rover," said Hamish, busily unwinding crime scene tape. "This whole area will need to be cordoned off. Give the clothes you have taken off to Constable Fraser and he will bag them up."

"Why?"

"Procedure," said Hamish, for he knew if Blair arrived on the scene, he would immediately consider this family as suspects.

Kylie eventually appeared wearing a low-cut red dress and very high heels.

"What are you tarted up for?" demanded Terence.

"The press and telly'll be here soon."

"They won't have time to get here," said Terence. "They won't hear of it until tomorrow."

Unfazed, Kylie said, "I'll phone the media as soon as we get out of here." She was the leading light of her local dramatic society and saw a golden opportunity to be propelled into that magic world of celebrities. Kylie had dreams of fame to make her forget the horror of the murder, but her husband and son still looked white and shaken.

After half an hour, when Dick had taken statements from the Hardy family, Hamish heard the sound in the sky of an approaching helicopter. He had one awful moment when he thought the police helicopter was going to land on the beach and maybe destroy any bit of evidence the killer might have left, but it landed on a flat bit of moorland behind the beach.

Blair climbed out followed by Jimmy Anderson, a policeman and policewoman, and a stocky man Hamish did not recognise.

"This here is the police surgeon, Mr. Carrick," said Blair. "Where's the body?"

"Down on the beach."

Blair stumped off followed by the surgeon. Hamish grabbed Jimmy's arm and whispered, "Cyril will have a mobile phone. Don't let Blair get it. I need proof that Blair sicced him onto me."

Before he reached Cyril's car, Blair turned round suddenly and shouted at Hamish, "You! Get back there. If those are the folk that found him, get their statement."

"I have all their statements," said Hamish.

"Just make sure they don't run off!"

Blair was desperate to search Cyril's body and make sure there was nothing on it to show that he was the one who had sent Cyril to chase Macbeth.

He was about to open the car door when Mr. Carrick pulled him back. "What are you doing, man? We can't do anything until a forensic team arrives. We should not even have come down to the crime scene."

So Blair returned to grill the Hardys until Terence shouted that he would get a lawyer and sue Blair for police harassment.

Blair turned his wrath on Hamish. "What were you doing up here anyway?"

"I got a report of a burglary."

"But there's nothing here!" roared Blair. "I looked down from the helicopter and couldn't see a single house."

"The voice was faint and I thought it might be a tourist who had something taken from his car," said Hamish.

The day dragged on. The forensic team arrived and the body had to be moved up the beach away from the rising tide. "Get down there," Hamish whispered urgently to

Jimmy, "and grab all the stuff Carrick will find in his pockets and get it before Blair. Dick, have you any alcohol?"

"I've a bottle of whisky I carry around. It helps to loosen up folk we might need to talk to."

"Give it to Blair."

"Are you mad? He'll drink the lot."

"That's the idea," said Hamish.

Blair accepted the whisky and a glass with a satisfied grunt. He felt he desperately needed something to quell his fears. Frightened that someone else might want some, he retreated to a flat rock and proceeded to make inroads into the bottle.

Soothed by the whisky and the susurration of the waves on the beach, Blair fell asleep, his heavy head on his chest.

The Hardys had been given permission to leave, and the first thing Kylie did when she once more got a phone signal was to call the press. She wanted to go back so that she could be photographed at the crime scene but her husband said grimly that he wasn't going back there.

Blair woke suddenly, blinked, and looked around. Jimmy Anderson was just coming up from the beach, carrying an evidence bag. "He was one of ours," said Jimmy. "Cyril Sessions."

The lights of a television camera crew suddenly flooded the scene. "I'll take that," said Blair, stumbling to his feet.

"Yes," said Jimmy loudly. "The dead man is policeman Cyril Sessions. I have his mobile phone here and his camera so we might find out who he was in contact with."

"Get oot o' here!" roared Blair, stumbling towards the television crew and waving his fists.

His heart sank as a long sleek car drew up and Superintendent Peter Daviot got out of the back.

"Do we have any identity for the dead man?" he asked.

"It's policeman Cyril Sessions," said Jimmy quickly. "I have his phone here along with other items. We can check it. Maybe he contacted the murderer before he died." He was wearing latex gloves. He fished out the phone.

"Leave it!" howled Blair. "We can check it back at headquarters."

"Give it to me," commanded Daviot. He drew out a pair of latex gloves and put them on. He switched on the phone and scrolled down the numbers Cyril had been phoning.

"There are calls to police headquarters and I recognise this one. Mr. Blair, this is your home phone number."

"I was training him," mumbled Blair. "Told him to keep in touch."

"Any text messages?" asked Hamish.

"Let me see. Yes, here is one. Good heavens! It is from you, Mr. Blair, and it says, 'Haven't you found out anything yet to nail that bastard Macbeth?' Mr. Blair, you will accompany me back to headquarters. Anderson, you are now in charge."

* * *

In vain did Blair protest that it was in the interests of the police to make sure Macbeth was doing his job. He was told he would be suspended from duty pending a full police enquiry.

Hetty Dunstable read of the death of Cyril in the morning paper and burst into tears. She was sure now that Cyril had loved her. Then she remembered Hamish saying he would shoot him.

Hamish went back the next morning on the road to Sandybeach, leaving Dick to man the police station and look after the dog and cat. He wished he had not switched off the siren as soon as he left the village the day before. Perhaps then more people would have come out of their cottages to watch. Cyril had been following him, but someone had been following Cyril.

Hamish stopped at cottages by the road to ask if anyone had seen cars going past. Two said they had seen the Land Rover, but no one had even seen Cyril's car following.

He knew a squad of police were scouring the ground all around the beach looking for clues. Hamish stopped by the side of the road to think.

He looked at the peaty moorland stretching on either side before the one-track road turned down to follow the coast. Perhaps the murderer had used a motorbike or dune buggy to come over the moors. Up on the moors, there was a good view of the road.

Hamish suddenly stood stock-still, assailed by a feeling

of dread. Thin black clouds were racing across the sky from the west, heralding a break in the good weather. From his vantage point up on the moors, he could see giant waves crashing down on the beach. He was just about to continue his search when he saw Dick's battered little Ford arriving along the road below and stopping beside the Land Rover. He sprinted down to meet him.

"You've to go straight to headquarters," said Dick. "Daviot's in a right taking."

"It's probably about this business of Blair getting Cyril to follow me," said Hamish.

Dick looked uneasy. "He seemed right furious with you. Do you want me to come with you?"

"Where are Sonsie and Lugs?"

"In the Land Rover."

"You look after them. I've probably got to write a report."

The fact that Daviot's secretary, Helen, greeted him with a welcome smile made Hamish uneasy. The only times that Helen had ever smiled on him were when he was in trouble.

After fifteen minutes, he was ushered in.

"This is terrible," said Daviot.

"Mr. Blair did this before. I mean, got someone to report on me."

"That is being dealt with. This latest thing is worse. We have received a phone call saying that you knew of Sessions's identity and said you would blow his head off."

"That would be the librarian, Hetty Dunstable," said Hamish. "She phoned me to say that she thought Sessions was spying on me because he kept asking her questions about me."

"She said you seemed aware of his identity."

"Sir, I was mildly irritated, that is all."

"I am sending men to the station to collect your guns for analysis. I want you to write a full report."

Hamish lost his temper, his face flaming as red as his hair. "I have worked hard as a police sergeant," he said. "I have never harmed anyone. If Sessions continued to annoy me, I would simply have sent in a report."

"Then write your report now," snapped Daviot. "You are suspended from duties until further enquiries."

Hamish went downstairs to the detectives' room where Jimmy Anderson was scowling at a computer screen.

"I heard the news," said Jimmy. "Who is this woman who's making all the trouble?"

"Hetty Dunstable. She's the librarian at Braikie library. She asked me to a party last year and came on to me. Took it bad when I didn't find her in the least attractive. This is spite. I'm suspended from duty. Now I've got to write a report."

"Go and do it from the police station," said Jimmy. "You can send it over."

"What worries me," said Hamish, "is the spin Blair will put on his behaviour. He'll try to justify the closing down of the police station, saying he was trying to save the force money. The only thing that's saved me so far is that no one else wants to police Sutherland. Has anyone searched Cyril's belongings?"

"Not yet. His only living relative is his mother. She's on her way up from Perth. I was just about to go there."

"I'd like a look at his stuff."

"You can't. You're suspended from duty."

"Just a wee look."

"Run along. But if anyone reports you, say you did it before you knew you were suspended."

The day had turned as grey as Hamish's mood. He parked the Land Rover at the police station and then walked along to Mrs. Mackenzie's as a fine drizzling rain began to fall, shrouding the mountains that loomed over the village.

Mrs. Mackenzie let Hamish into the house, demanding to know when she could let the room again.

"Och, you'll need to wait until detectives have looked around as well."

Grumbling under her breath, Mrs. Mackenzie unlocked the door to Cyril's room.

Hamish walked in and shut the door in her face. He pulled on a pair of latex gloves and went straight to Cyril's backpack, which was lying in a corner.

It was closed with a small padlock. He took out a Swiss knife and, selecting the thinnest blade, sprang the lock. He searched through a jumble of socks, underwear, and sweaters. There seemed to be nothing of interest. No notebook or photographs. He opened the curtained cubicle which served as wardrobe. Two jackets, two pairs of trousers, and an anorak were hanging there. He searched the pockets without finding even a receipt. Two pairs of trainers and a pair of black shoes were lying on the floor. In one of the trainers, he found a slip of paper. A Strathbane phone number was scrawled on it.

There was no sign of a camera or a computer. Hamish pushed back his cap and scratched his fiery hair. There must be something in Cyril's life to have prompted his murder.

He looked down from the window. Jimmy was just climbing out of a car with another detective. Two policemen drew up in a car behind them.

Hamish put the slip of paper in his pocket, left the room, ran along the passage outside, pushed open a fire door at the end, and made his way down to the back garden. He scaled the garden wall and made his way to the police station over the fields at the back.

Dick was standing in the kitchen, mixing something up in a bowl with a wooden spoon while the dog and cat looked up at him hopefully.

"I hear you've been suspended," said Dick.

"Who told you?"

"Copper friend o' mine."

"What are you doing?"

"I'm trying my hand at scones," said Dick. "The Currie sisters gave me their recipe."

Hamish half closed his eyes. It should be a pretty woman standing there with the mixing bowl. Not some chubby policeman.

"Leave it," he said. "There's a librarian at Braikie, Hetty Dunstable. She landed me in this mess. She told headquarters I had threatened to shoot Cyril. I think she's got a spite against me because I spurned her advances."

Dick grinned. "That's an old-fashioned way o' putting it. Did you cast her off like a worn-out glove?"

"Whatever. Look, no one said anything about you being suspended, so get over there and see if you can charm her into repairing the damage."

"What about my scones?"

Hamish told him crudely where to put his scones, and Dick slammed down the bowl and left in a huff.

When Hamish had finished typing up his report, he took out the slip of paper he had found in Cyril's trainer and looked at it. He should have left it where it was for Jimmy to find, but he was angry at being suspended and wanted to show Strathbane that Hamish Macbeth was too valuable a policeman to be kept off the case.

Then he thought, if the phone number led to anything, he would need to explain where he got it. He could always say he found it outside the police station after Cyril had taken that photograph. But it was raining and the paper was dry. His face cleared. Archie Maclean could always say he found it on his boat and passed it on to Hamish.

He read over his report and began to feel uneasy. What if they checked the police station phone to make sure he had really been called out and had not been luring Cyril to a remote spot to bump him off?

He put a fresh tape in his answering machine. Disguising his voice and speaking in Gaelic, he gave yesterday's date and a time of ten minutes past nine. He would give Jimmy the tape and hope that his phone would not be further investigated.

He then dialled the operator, identified himself, and gave the phone number on the slip of paper, asking for the name and address belonging to the number. The operator said she would call him back for security reasons, to make sure he really was who he said he was.

Hamish waited patiently. When the phone rang, he seized it. "The number is that of an M. Bentley, Number Fifteen, Sheep Street, Strathbane," she said. Hamish thanked her and then got out a street map of Strathbane. Sheep Street was in the old part of town, a nucleus of little streets off the main shopping area.

He knew he should really pass this information on to Jimmy, but his highland curiosity was demanding that he find out for himself.

He changed out of his uniform into civilian clothes. He called on Archie Maclean, who agreed to say the paper had been found on his boat. Dick had taken the Land Rover, so, telling Sonsie and Lugs to stay behind and behave themselves, he got into Dick's old car and set out for Strathbane.

Dick parked outside the library and went in. A pretty girl was stacking the shelves. Dick approached her. "Miss Dunstable?"

"Not me," she said. "I'm just the assistant. Hetty's off today. She's awfy upset at her boyfriend being murdered."

"I'll need to be having a wee word with her," said Dick. "Give me the lassie's address."

"She's got a wee bungalow on the shore road. It's called Atlantic View. She got it on the cheap 'cos no one wants to live there."

"Why not? It used to be flooded but now they've got that new seawall."

"Aye, but the waves are higher every year and folk say the wall isn't high enough. Last winter, the waves got over it twice."

"What's your name?" asked Dick.

"Shona Macdonald."

"Get on all right with Miss Dunstable?"

"Aye. She really loves books. When it's quiet, she reads the whole time."

"What does she read?" Shona had large blue eyes in a little heart-shaped face.

Wish I wasn't so old, thought Dick ruefully.

"She likes romances, but the old-fashioned kind. Hearts and flowers. No *Fifty Shades of Grey*. She thought that book was disgusting and tried to have it banned. But she couldn't because a lot of people wanted it. When the provost's wife asked for a copy, I thought Hetty was going to burst into tears."

"I'll be having a word with her," said Dick. Those eyes of Shona's were so very blue, like Lochdubh on a summer's day.

"Isn't it boring work for a pretty girl like you?" he asked.

"Oh, no," said Shona. "I read a lot and I like chatting to people. It's not usually so quiet as this." She glanced at the clock. "I'd better lock up. It's my lunch hour."

"I'm feeling a wee bit peckish," said Dick. "Fancy a bite to eat?"

"All right. I usually go to Jean's café next door. She's got good mutton pies and not the shop ones, either."

"Sounds great," said Dick. He told himself he was only doing his job. The more he could find out about Hetty before actually meeting her, the better. But when Shona collected her coat and handbag and locked up the library, he noticed the sun had come out and was shining on her glossy black curls, and he felt his fifty-one years melting away and suddenly he was young again.

Chapter Three

*There's no art
To find the mind's construction in the face.*
                                        —Shakespeare

Sheep Street appeared to be in the throes of gentrification. At the corner, the bakery was selling croissants. Croissants always came just before the builders, reflected Hamish. In fact, people sometimes talked of their area being "croissantified."

It was a small street with sandstone villas on either side. Builders were working on a few, and others had several doorbells, showing where the villas had been cut into small flats. Hamish was surprised that there was enough money in financially depressed Strathbane to gentrify anything.

He found the address he was looking for. This villa had been recently renovated. There was only one doorbell at the side of a gleaming black-painted door embellished with a large brass lion's-head knocker.

Hamish rang the bell. The door was opened by a tall woman with long straight brown hair, high cheekbones, and eyes as grey as the North Sea.

"Do you know a policeman called Cyril Sessions?" asked Hamish.

"Who are you?"

Her accent was Scottish. Because of her appearance, Hamish had expected her to have an Eastern European accent.

He produced his warrant card, which Daviot had neglected to confiscate. "I am a policeman from Lochdubh," he said. "I am investigating the murder of Cyril Sessions. He had a note of your phone number."

"Why aren't you in uniform?"

"Plainclothes," said Hamish, desperately beginning to wish he had turned his information over to Jimmy. "Who are you?"

"I am Anna Eskdale. I work for Mr. Bentley."

"May I speak to Mr. Bentley?"

"Wait there. I will see if he is available."

She shut the door. Hamish waited patiently. A watery sunlight was gilding the cobbles, and the air was full of the noise of builders' radios and grinding machinery.

A seagull landed on the ground at Hamish's feet and surveyed him with prehistoric eyes. "Go away. I havenae anything for you," said Hamish.

"Do you usually talk to the birds?"

Hamish swung round. Anna had quietly reopened the door. "Mr. Bentley will see you now."

He followed her down a narrow passage and into a study at the back. A plump middle-aged man sat behind an antique desk. He had thinning hair combed over a pink scalp and small pale blue eyes half buried in creases of fat. The study was lined with books from floor to ceiling.

"I am Murdo Bentley," he said. "I gather you are the policeman from Lochdubh."

"Yes, I am investigating Cyril Sessions's murder. He had your phone number in his belongings."

"I do not read the newspapers," he said. "Was he a good-looking man?"

"Yes."

"I think that would be the policeman who called here a few weeks ago. He said that there had been a report that someone in Sheep Street was dealing drugs and asked if I knew anything. I said I travelled a lot and did not know my neighbours, the few that are left."

"What is your job?" asked Hamish, moving from foot to foot. Murdo was in the only chair.

"I am a restaurateur. I own the Seven Steps outside Strathbane."

Hamish recalled that the Seven Steps was a very expensive restaurant, popular for weddings and conventions.

He felt uneasy. The study was very quiet. He thought there must be some sort of soundproofing as no noise from

outside filtered into the room. Also, in depressed Strathbane, there was a gulf between the haves and have-nots, and
the haves were a small group who mostly knew each other.
Daviot belonged to the haves.

"If you do hear of anything, let me know," said Hamish.

The door opened and Anna appeared. Hamish thought
that Murdo must have pressed some sort of bell or buzzer
on his desk, possibly just under his desk.

"Show the constable out," said Murdo.

Over lunch, Shona told Dick that she had been at Hetty's
party when Hetty had got drunk and had thrown herself at
Hamish. "She told us all afterwards that Macbeth had been
coming on to her," said Shona. "None of us believed her."

"Does she tell lies?" asked Dick.

"Only when it comes to men. She thinks everything in
trousers fancies her. When she began to talk about Cyril,
well, we all thought she was fantasising until we saw them
one evening in the pub and he had his hand on her knee and
Hetty looked as if she'd just won the lottery. I still wonder
what he saw in her."

"He was spying on Hamish," said Dick.

"Why?"

"There's this awful detective inspector in Strathbane who
wants proof to close down the police station."

"Poor Hetty. Look, thanks for lunch. I'd better get back."

"Maybe we could do this again?"

"That would be nice. Got to rush."

Dick held open the café door for her. He felt as if his whole body were smiling.

Then he remembered he was supposed to see Hetty.

Atlantic View was a box of a bungalow set on a rise above the shore road. There was no garden, just a fenced-off area of shaggy grass. The tide was up, and great waves were dashing themselves against the seawall. The air was full of the sound of the sea and the screeching of gulls. Dick had read that the gull population was falling fast. He detested the birds. With the depleted fishing stocks, the marauding birds were known to steal food out of the hands of people, trying to eat fish-and-chips or ice cream. Hadn't a small child over at the Kyle of Lochalsh only the other day had an ice cream cone snatched from its fingers?

He rang the bell and waited. Hetty answered the door. She looked at Dick's uniform and put a hand to her thin chest. Her prominent eyes welled up with tears. "Is it about poor Cyril?"

"If I could just be having a word," said Dick, removing his cap.

"I've seen you on the telly, haven't I?" said Hetty, ushering him into the house. "You've been on quiz shows."

"Yes, that's me."

The living room into which she led him seemed to be a sort of shrine to Hetty. Framed photographs of her hung on the walls and stood on nests of little tables. A one-bar electric heater stood in front of the empty fireplace. There was a three-piece suite of white imitation leather standing on a white shag carpet. A low coffee table held a series of celebrity magazines.

Dick was urged to sit down. Hetty perched on the edge of an armchair opposite him.

"I am here to find out why you said that Hamish Macbeth had threatened to shoot Cyril Sessions," said Dick. "You became suspicious of Cyril when he asked so many questions about Macbeth and told Hamish. He was irritated and made that remark off the top of his head. Why on earth did you tell Strathbane?"

"I thought Hamish had become jealous," said Hetty.

"Miss Dunstable, I have asked questions about your connection to Hamish. It appears that you got drunk at a party, came on to him, and he rebuffed you. Hamish has now been suspended from duty so I need to gather evidence to clear his name. By the time all my witnesses have made their statements, you will look very bad indeed. How, the authorities will ask you, can Hamish Macbeth have been jealous when he had no romantic feelings towards you at all?"

"But he did threaten to shoot Cyril!"

"Of course, if you were to telephone headquarters and say Hamish was only joking or something like that, I would not need to investigate further."

She stared at him with a sulky expression. "Hamish led me on."

"I think your imagination led you on," said Dick severely. "My God, lassie, if Hamish loses his job and his police station for the likes of you, I'll damn well crucify you and so will every other copper in the Highlands."

Hetty began to cry until she saw her tears were having no effect on Dick whatsoever.

"Cyril did love me," she said at last.

"Oh, aye? Then what made you suspicious?"

"At first he swept me off my feet. Then he began to ask question after question about Hamish. I finally said I was sick of the subject and wouldn't talk about Hamish any more. That was when he stopped seeing me or answering my calls."

"Have you a computer here?" asked Dick.

"Yes, I've got a laptop."

"Get it in here and write out a statement. You are going to confess that you reported Hamish out of spite."

"I can't do that!"

"It's either that or I'll make your life a misery. I have friends in the press. Want to see your name in the papers?"

Statement secured, Dick headed straight for police headquarters and demanded to see Daviot.

"Have you an appointment?" asked Helen.

"I have not, but this is of the utmost importance," said Dick.

Helen disappeared into the inner office. She returned after a few moments and said curtly, "You're to go in."

"What is it?" demanded Daviot when Dick stood meekly in front of his desk.

"Just this," said Dick, and handed over Hetty Dunstable's statement.

"This is dreadful," he said.

"Now, that is why I brought it to you," said Dick. "You'll be anxious to get some damage limitation."

"Damage limitation?"

"Wouldn't it be awful, sir, if it got out to the press that Hamish Macbeth was suspended from duty due to the spite of one woman? It would also have to come out that Cyril Sessions lost his life while he was spying on Hamish for Mr. Blair."

Hamish was on the road back to Lochdubh to confess to Jimmy about that slip of paper when his mobile rang. He pulled into the side of the road to answer it.

It was Daviot. "There has been a grave misunderstanding, Macbeth. You are back on duty. That is all. You are to say nothing of Mr. Blair's connection to Sessions until the matter is cleared up."

"Yes, sir," said Hamish. "What…?"

But Daviot had rung off.

Hamish's phone rang again. It was Mr. Patel, Lochdubh's shopkeeper. "Hamish, there are a couple o' scientists from Strathbane University. They've heard you've got a wild cat and since the beasties are that rare, they want to take Sonsie away for DNA tests. We all said it was nothing but a big black cat and they'll be back tomorrow. You'd better dye the cat black. I've got the right hair dye in the shop. It won't hurt the beast."

Hamish thanked him, but after he had rung off, he cursed the interfering scientists.

When he got to the police station, it was to find that Dick had already collected the dye. "You're going to have to do it yourself, Hamish," he said. "I doubt if Sonsie would let anyone else near."

"This is a right mess," said Hamish. "I should have guessed that something like this would happen sooner or later. Wild cats, they say, are nearly extinct. They'd chust love to get their hands on one. I cannae see poor Sonsie allowing even me to dye her fur. Get her up to the Tommel Castle Hotel tomorrow. Angela Brodie's got a big black cat. I'll borrow that. I'll pay you for the dye."

"Leave it. I might use it myself," said Dick. "Grey hair is awfy ageing."

Hamish eyed him narrowly. "Oh, aye? And who is she?"

Dick blushed. "There's no one. I just thought I'd look better."

"Suit yourself. So how did you get on with Hetty?"

"I got her to sign a statement saying she had lied to get back at you and I took it to Daviot."

"Thanks. I owe you a lot."

The kitchen door opened, and Jimmy walked in. "I got a call that you're no longer suspended," he said. "Got any whisky?"

Hamish took a bottle and glass down from a cupboard. "I've got a bit of news for you, Jimmy. Have a drink first."

Jimmy poured himself a hefty measure, took a swallow, and then asked, "What have you been up to?"

Hamish told him about the phone number and his visit to Murdo Bentley. "I tried to phone you," he lied. "But you must have been in a black area. It didn't seem that important because it was just a wee bit o' paper Archie Maclean found on his boat. It could have come from a tourist."

"Sheep Street," said Jimmy. "I'll check up. I cannae remember anything to do wi' drugs in Sheep Street. I'll look into that."

"Do you think some drug gang might have decided to murder Cyril?"

"I cannae remember Cyril being involved in any drugs case, unless it was when I was on holiday. I'll let you know. I'll go and see this Murdo Bentley myself. I've heard o' him. Owns the Seven Steps restaurant. Some soap star had her wedding there last year. Does good works. Set up a boys' club down at the docks. Gives a lot to charity."

"Is he married?"

"Cannae recall."

"He's got some sort of assistant, Anna Eskdale. Ring any bells?"

"No. Look, Hamish, the man's a pillar of the community."

"Still, it's odd that…" Hamish broke off. He had been about to say that it was odd Cyril had kept that phone number hidden in one of his trainers. "I mean, why did Cyril have a note of that one phone number?"

"You say Archie found it on his boat. It may not have come from Cyril. Could have been dropped by a tourist. Anyway, thanks for the dram. We've asked around the village here. No one saw anyone following Cyril when he left for Sandybeach."

After Jimmy had left, Hamish walked along to Angela Brodie's cottage. The doctor's wife was, as usual, scowling at her laptop on the kitchen table. "Looking for inspiration?" asked Hamish.

"I'm looking up frock shops."

"Why?"

"My last book was a detective story. Didn't I give you a copy?"

"No. What's it called?"

"*A Very Highland Murder*. Got good reviews and I've been nominated for an award. My agent says it's full evening dress. It's going to be televised. The event is sponsored by Bramley Sofas. There are to be awards for different categories of fiction. It's for new writers."

"But you're not a new writer."

"I wrote it under another name. I'm a new detective writer."

"Where is it being held?"

"At the Seven Steps restaurant."

"Now, there's a coincidence. I was just interviewing the owner today. Haven't you got an evening gown?"

"It's an old thing. I must wear something special. Ah,

here's something. Jessie's Bridal and Evening Wear. Inverness. I might try them."

"When is it?"

"Next month. The thirtieth."

"Angela, I need to borrow your black cat."

"Why? Can't you dye Sonsie?"

"You've heard about these scientists?"

"The whole village has heard about them, Hamish. I'll bring Sooty over in the morning, but be kind to her and don't let Lugs frighten her."

Sooty was delivered the next morning. She was a very large, fat lazy cat who ignored Lugs. Dick, with his newly dyed moustache and dyed hair, took Sonsie off to the Tommel Castle Hotel. Clarry, the cook, welcomed Dick and praised him on his new look. "Takes years off you," he said. "Like something to eat?"

"I'm on a diet," said Dick. "Well, maybe a wee bit o' toast."

Lugs barked at Sooty and had to be shut up in the bedroom. The scientists arrived: a tall, thin, elderly man and a short, round bossy woman.

"Let's see it!" she demanded.

"For heffen's sakes," said Hamish crossly. "This is also my home. You don't just barge in making demands without pausing to draw a breath. I want identification for a start."

Grumbling, they produced driving licenses which Hamish examined with maddening slowness.

Then he said, "The cat's through here."

He led them into the living room where Sooty was asleep in front of the fire.

The woman scientist glared at him. "That's not a wild cat!"

"I never said it was," said Hamish.

"But we had a report that you were keeping a wild cat."

"Aye, Sooty can be a handful if she's riled up."

"Come along, Brenda," said the man. "Another false lead."

When they had left, Hamish followed them out and watched until their car had disappeared out of the village. He went back indoors and collected Sooty and returned her to Angela.

"You can't keep Sonsie hidden forever," said Angela. "Have you thought of returning her to the wild?"

"There was no reason afore with the beast being happy wi' me."

"Do you think I should wear a wig?"

"What!"

"For the awards." Angela tugged fretfully at her wispy hair.

"Why don't you just go as yourself?" said Hamish. "Nothing up with you."

"I'd like to shine, just once."

"Get your hair done, then."

"I'll think about it."

* * *

Hamish returned to the police station, collected his dog, and drove up to the Tommel Castle Hotel. He was just getting down from the Land Rover when he saw a familiar blonde head in the gift shop and his heart gave a lurch.

He walked to the shop and opened the door. Priscilla Halburton-Smythe was arranging goods on the shelves. "Back again," said Hamish.

She swung round, and her face lit up when she saw him. "I've got some holiday due to me and the woman who works here is off sick so I'm filling in. Are you working on that policeman's murder?"

"Trying to."

"I'm closing up for lunch," said Priscilla. "Why don't you join me and tell me all about it?"

"That'll be grand. I've just got to find Dick. He's hiding out in the hotel with Sonsie."

"I heard about the scientists. How did you get on?"

Hamish told her as she locked up and they walked together into the hotel. The manager, Mr. Johnson, told Hamish that Dick was in the kitchen. "I'll meet you in the dining room," said Priscilla.

In the kitchen, Hamish bent down and stroked Sonsie's soft fur. "I'm having lunch with Priscilla," he told Dick. "You can join us if you like."

"I'm on a diet," said Dick.

"Since when?"

"Since today," said Dick. "I'll take the beasts back to the station and phone you if Jimmy turns up."

In the dining room, Priscilla listened as Hamish told her all about Cyril. When he had finished, she asked, "This Murdo Bentley? What did you make of him?"

"It's hard to know," said Hamish. "It was an odd sort of house. There's building going on all around but his study was so quiet. Probably soundproofed or triple glazing. I would have expected a successful businessman like him to have a house in the country."

"Maybe he has," said Priscilla. "Or a flat at the restaurant. It's a big place. There's a restaurant, a brasserie, and suites that are used for wedding receptions and conventions. I tell you what, let's have dinner in the brasserie tonight."

"All right," said Hamish. "What time?"

"Pick me up at seven thirty and I'll book a table for eight."

"It's that phone number that puzzles me. I told Jimmy it had been found on Archie Maclean's boat but I found it in one of Cyril's trainers. Now, why would he keep that number if Murdo was only just a man he had interviewed?"

"We'll get a feel of the place anyway," said Priscilla.

Hamish returned to the police station followed by Dick, to be confronted by an angry Jimmy Anderson. "Where the hell have you been?" he demanded.

"I was finding out a bit more about Murdo Bentley," said Hamish.

"Well, forget it," snapped Jimmy. "The pair of you get back up to the location of Sandybeach. I want every man combing the whole area."

Hamish and Dick set off in the Land Rover with Sonsie and Lugs in the back. Hamish did not want to leave his pets behind because there was a large flap on the police station door allowing them to come and go and he didn't want the cat to be seen wandering around the village to be spotted by any cruising scientist.

It has been said of Sutherland that you can experience five climates in one day. A blustery wind had sprung up, whipping up choppy waves on the Atlantic and singing in the heather.

Hamish turned off the road before they got to Sandybeach and started bumping over the moorland. "Where are we going?" asked Dick.

"I've a feeling that whoever murdered Cyril might have come over the back way on a motorbike. No one in the cottages on the road up said they saw anyone other than Cyril, the Hardys, and then us in the Land Rover."

"They've asked around Lochdubh," said Dick. "No one saw anyone watching the police station or Mrs. Mackenzie's."

"Say someone was on a motorbike or a dune buggy," said Hamish, "all they would have to do was park up on a rise on the moorland overlooking the village. That way they would see Cyril setting off."

"Maybe," said Dick. "But they would see us first and then Cyril following. Who would want to murder Cyril with the police around?"

"I don't know," said Hamish, bringing the Land Rover to a stop. "But say someone had a vantage point where they could see us going past Sandybeach and Cyril turning down to the place."

"You'd think we would have heard the shot," said Cyril.

"Where we picnicked was sheltered by the cliffs around and the noise of the waves and the seagulls might have drowned the sound. Okay, let's get out and start searching. Up here is where you can see anyone arriving at the beach."

"It's pretty impossible wi' all this heather," grumbled Dick.

"Keep looking. There might be a damp patch somewhere."

The breeze died down and the sun was warm. Sonsie and Lugs chased each other through the heather. Dick began to dream about Shona Macdonald. Did his dyed hair and moustache really make him look younger? Maybe if he lost a few stone in weight, he could lose years in appearance.

"Got something!" called Hamish, interrupting his dream.

Dick hurried to join him.

Where the heather had thinned out, there was a damp patch of ground with a tyre track across it. "Looks like a motorbike," said Hamish, taking out his phone. He called

Jimmy and told him to get someone over immediately to make a plaster cast of the track.

Once a cast of the track had been taken, searching policemen moved away from the beach area and spread out over the moors.

Dick's stomach gave out a grumbling noise. "I suppose you're hungry," said Hamish. "We'll look around a bit more and then get something to eat. Did you bring anything?"

"No," said Dick curtly.

Hamish studied him thoughtfully. Dyed hair and moustache and no food? What was going on?

"I didnae find Hetty attractive," commented Hamish cautiously.

"Neither did I," said Dick crossly.

"So what's wi' the dyed hair and not eating?"

"I just felt like it. Okay?"

"Well, let's search a bit more."

Dick walked away, his head bowed, searching the ground. At last Hamish said, "If you don't want to eat, I do." He phoned Jimmy and said they were taking a break.

Hamish drove to the hotel at Scourie. It was built by the second Duke of Sutherland as a coaching inn and stood on the site of an old fortified house. Hamish and Dick found a table in the dining room. Outside were the white sands of Scourie Bay and the gable-stepped houses of Scourie village. Dick's stomach gave a fierce rumble as he looked dismally out at the distant tops of Ben Stack, Foinaven, and Arkle.

"I might just have a roll and butter," said Dick miserably.

"Look here," said Hamish, "I've noticed the ladies like you chust the way you are."

"What have ladies got to do with it?" demanded Dick.

"Everything, I would say," said Hamish.

"Well, they haven't!"

"There's nothing folk hate more than a bad-tempered man," said Hamish. "And without food, you're a menace. Here's the waiter. Order something, and cheer up!"

Dick gave in and ploughed his way through three hearty courses. They were just enjoying their coffee in the lounge when Hamish's phone rang. It was Jimmy. "Would you believe it?" he yelled. "Blair's back."

"Nothing to be done to him for spying on me?" asked Hamish.

"Daviot said he was only doing his duty as a conscientious officer of the law."

"Well, I'll be damned," said Hamish.

"You will, too, if Blair has anything to do with it. He's up here, raging around like a mad bull and demanding to know where you are."

"We're further ower towards Braikie," said Hamish. "We'll come and join you. Found anything else?"

"Nothing, and the weather looks bad."

"Be with you as fast as we can."

Hamish looked out of the window. The sky had clouded over the vista of lochs and mountains that made up the empty quarter of Sutherland. He paid the bill and reluctantly left the hotel as the rain was beginning to fall.

By the time they reached the area around Sandybeach, it was to find it deserted. Hamish phoned Jimmy. "Blair said we couldn't do anything further because of the rain, but he says you're to stay up there and keep on looking."

"Malicious scunner," said Hamish after he had rung off and conveyed the latest news to Dick. "It's coming down in torrents now. Let's go back to Scourie and have some more coffee in case Blair checks at the station in Lochdubh."

They returned to Lochdubh after they considered the road home to be safe from Blair skulking around.

As Hamish was preparing to go out that evening, Dick wondered whether he might just take a trip to Braikie. Perhaps, if he were lucky, he might see Shona walking down the street. *Oh, hullo*, he would say, ever so casual. In his imagination her face would light up. *What about a bit o' supper?* he'd suggest. Soon they would be seated at a candlelit table and...

"What are you smiling at?" asked Hamish.

"I was only thinking of a clever question for a quiz," said Dick hurriedly. "I might write a book for pub quizzes."

"Aren't there a lot of them?"

"But I've got the name. In fact, there doesn't seem to be any chance of me being allowed on a TV quiz show again. Strathbane Television said it spoilt the excitement for the viewers when everybody knew I was going to win."

"I'm off, then," said Hamish.

He was wearing his one good suit, and his red hair had

been brushed until it shone like a flame in the kitchen light.

"Have fun," said Dick.

He waited until he heard Hamish drive off and then changed out of his uniform into a blazer, flannels, white shirt, and silk tie. Dick was heading out the door when he realised that Sonsie and Lugs were following him. Dick cursed under his breath. If he left them behind, they could get out through the flap and would probably head for the Italian restaurant. Hamish would no doubt get to hear of it.

He gloomily let them into the back of his car. "I'm nothing more than an animal keeper," he grumbled.

Dick had forgotten how empty Braikie could be in the evening. He drove slowly up the main street and then took to the side streets, always looking to left and right in the hope he might catch a glimpse of Shona.

At last he drove back to the main street and parked the car. The dog and cat shifted restlessly in the back. His conscience pricked him. How old was Shona? Late twenties. What sort of policeman was he? He hadn't looked for a wedding ring or even an engagement ring.

"Come on, beasties," he said, letting the dog and cat out. "I'll get you some fish-and-chips."

Fortified with a large packet of fish-and-chips and a bottle of Irn-Bru, Dick felt as if he had been restored to sanity. What on earth had he been thinking of? He had just turned fifty-one.

He gathered up the greasy papers—Sonsie had enjoyed a fish and Lugs, a deep-fried haggis slice—and crossed to a waste bin. Then he froze. Beside the waste bin was a pub, and as he was about to turn away, the door opened and Shona emerged with a handsome young man.

"Why it's yourself!" cried Shona. "What are you doing in Braikie?"

"Just checking the streets," said Dick, "but it all seems quiet."

"Are those your animals?" Sonsie and Lugs had crossed the road and were staring up at her.

"They're Hamish Macbeth's," said Dick. "He's out tonight so I'm stuck with them."

"What a magnificent cat! It's very big."

"Looks just like a wild cat," said her companion.

"No, no," said Dick quickly. "Just big."

"I'm sorry," said Shona. "I forgot to introduce you. This is my brother, Kelvin. Kelvin, this is that nice policeman, Mr. Fraser, that I told you about."

Dick heartily shook Kelvin's hand. Her brother! He glanced down at her hands. There was a garnet ring on the fourth finger of her right hand. No engagement ring, no wedding ring. All his good resolutions disappeared and his heart sang.

Hamish and Priscilla entered the brasserie. The room was dark, lit only with single candles on each table.

Priscilla was wearing a black sheath dress and high heels.

Hamish saw the men casting admiring glances in her direction. He often wondered why she was still single. Perhaps potential suitors were put off by her sexual coldness. It was that coldness that had made him break off their engagement. And yet, part of him still longed for a passionate Priscilla that did not exist.

Hamish peered at the menu. "The prices are pretty steep," he said. "I thought the brasserie was supposed to be cheaper than the dining room."

"I'm paying," said Priscilla.

"Oh, no you're not," said Hamish huffily. "The place is crowded. I don't know how they can all afford it."

"It's a special offer evening. Get the waiter to take away the à la carte menu and bring us the set menu."

When the set menu appeared, it turned out to be only twenty-five pounds a head. "I saw this menu advertised in the *Highland Times* before we left," said Priscilla. "It looks not bad."

The menu offered a choice of two starters: venison pâté or cock-a-leekie soup. The main dishes were either braised kidneys or roast chicken and the dessert: sherry trifle or chocolate gâteau. Probably the cheapest ingredients they could think of, thought Hamish.

At Priscilla's urging, he ordered a carafe of red wine instead of one of the bottles on offer, because the prices were outrageous.

While they ate venison pâté and braised kidneys, Pricilla talked about gossip from the hotel and Hamish half listened while stretching his policeman's antennae round the room. But it was all very middle-class highland Scottish. It was hard to make out people clearly in the dimness. Hamish had a good memory for villains and a good nose for smelling out the ones who had so far flown beneath the radar. But all seemed so respectable.

After they had finished their coffee, Hamish said, "Well, thanks for the idea, Priscilla, but I can't get even one sniff of wrongdoing."

He called for the bill. Then his eyes sharpened. "What's up?" asked Priscilla.

"Something's odd. The waiter went to ring up our bill and the maître d' said something to him and picked up the phone. The waiter stopped trying to get the bill."

"Is your credit card maxed out?" asked Priscilla.

"No, I didn't give it to him. I was waiting for him to bring his machine over to the table."

They waited. Then Hamish gave an impatient noise and made to rise to his feet. The maître d' came hurrying over. "Mr. Macbeth," he said with a smile. "Our owner, Mr. Bentley, says that you are our guests for the evening."

"I'm sorry," said Hamish. "I am a policeman and I can't accept freebies. Thank him very much but bring me the bill right away."

"But, sir…"

"Do as you're told," snapped Hamish.

Priscilla looked amused. "Hamish Macbeth, the famous moocher of the Highlands, turning down a free meal!"

"This is great," said Hamish. "Did you book the table under my name?"

"No, under mine."

"There is probably a CCTV camera somewhere scanning the guests so that Bentley can know who is in his restaurant. I wonder if Cyril ate here."

The bill arrived. Hamish scanned it to make sure he was being charged for everything and then paid.

In the car on the road back, Priscilla said, "Maybe he was just being generous. Surely a lot of these places like to cosy up to the police for security reasons."

"Maybe, but this stinks, somehow. Murdo Bentley gave me the creeps. I wonder if he's offered free hospitality to anyone other than Cyril, like Blair or Daviot."

"Wouldn't they refuse just like you?"

"Not if Murdo was a member of their lodge or Rotary Club. We all help each other, type of thing. Daviot wouldn't see anything wrong with it if that were the case. The well-heeled of Strathbane are a very small community."

"How are you going to go with this?"

"I don't know. I'll talk it over with Jimmy."

Hamish arrived home to find that Dick had shaved off his moustache. He was lounging in a sofa in the living room with the large cat draped over his lap like a rug and the dog at his feet. Sonsie opened one eye, looked at Hamish, and went back to sleep again.

"Can I get you something?" asked Dick.

"No, I'm fine. Why did you shave off your moustache?"

"Felt like a change. I think I'll let the black hair grow out."

"Good idea," said Hamish. He thought Dick's face looked almost babyish and naked without the moustache.

He went through to the police office and phoned Jimmy. Jimmy listened to Hamish's suspicions about Murdo.

"I can't really see us doing anything about it," said Jimmy. "The man's as clean as a whistle. I think you're out on a limb there, Hamish. But we may have a lead. Sam's Rides over at Dornoch reported the theft of a motorbike four days ago."

"What make?"

"A Honda CB1000."

"What time of day did the theft take place?"

"Bang in the middle of the day. One of the staff had been letting a customer go for a test drive. They went into the office to get out the paperwork. The idiot salesman left the keys in the ignition. Next thing they know someone in leathers and a helmet roared off with it. Get over there tomorrow and have a word with them."

"What about the autopsy?"

"Pretty much what the killing looked like—a shotgun blast to the chest."

"Okay, Jimmy, I'll go there tomorrow."

"Have you interviewed that librarian?"

"Dick spoke to her. Cyril bedded her and then left her flat. Dick got her to sign a statement saying she had lied about me which is why I'm back on the job. Didn't Daviot tell you?"

"I was told by Helen that you were to be given a second chance."

"Bitches to the right o' me and bitches to the left o' me," said Hamish moodily.

"And tell Dick to get back to the library and talk to Hetty again. See if she had any inkling that Cyril was on drugs."

"Anything been found in his blood?"

"They're checking. It isn't *CSI: Miami*. It's Scotland. Takes forever."

The following morning, Hamish told Dick he was to go to the library to talk once more to Hetty.

Dick looked elated. "Glad to," he said.

"You're not sweet on Hetty, are you?"

"No! You have to be joking."

Dick retreated to look out his best uniform, one he hardly ever wore, considering it wasted on the usual sort of jobs he was asked to perform. When he emerged it was to find that Hamish had left and had taken the dog and cat with him.

He set off for Braikie on a sunny day. The sky above was clear blue and the two mountains that loomed over the village had a covering of snow on their peaks.

Dick was in such a good mood that he even stopped on the waterfront to say good morning to the Currie sisters.

"What have you done to your hair?" asked Nessie.

"Hair?" echoed her sister.

"It grows in black from time to time," said Dick defensively.

"Nonsense. That's one bad dye job," said Nessie.

"Bad dye job," murmured Jessie.

Dick let in the clutch and roared off, his face flaming. The dye was supposed to be temporary and wash out after several shampoos. Dick got as far as the Tommel Castle Hotel when he suddenly made a U-turn and raced back to the police station. Once inside, he stripped off, went into the shower, and shampooed his hair vigorously as rivulets of black dye coursed down his plump body. He finally towelled his hair dry and saw to his relief that most of the dye had gone.

But the exercise of having to race back to the police station to get rid of the dye had sobered his elation. He vowed to be sensible. Shona was not for him. He would do his duty and talk to the horrible Hetty. He reflected that maybe Blair had some sort of hold over Cyril. Otherwise, why would an Adonis like Cyril go so far as to seduce Hetty?

Chapter Four

Come, and take a choice of all my library,
And so beguile thy sorrow.

—Shakespeare

Hamish arrived at Sam's Rides in Dornoch. It was on the outskirts of the town. Sam Buchan, the owner, seemed pleased to see him. He was a big highlander with a shock of grey hair and hands like spades.

"I thocht the police had forgotten about thon theft," he said. "Cheeky sod. Nipped the bike from under ma nose."

"Do you have CCTV?" asked Hamish.

"Aye. I kept thon tape. Come into the office and have a look."

Hamish's heart sank when he saw the tape. It must have been used over and over again and it was like looking at the film through a snowstorm. A dim figure in helmet and leathers mounted the bike and roared off.

"Did you ask in the town if anyone had seen this biker on foot?"

"Nobody saw anything."

Hamish walked out of the office and looked around. Across the road from the business was a stand of trees. "I'll look over there," he said. "Someone could have hidden in those trees and waited for an opportunity."

He walked over and began to search the ground. He found two cigarette butts and put them in a forensic bag. Looking across the road, he could understand why Sam and his employees didn't bother much about security. It looked so quiet and peaceful. Above Dornoch, on the top of snow-covered Ben Bhraggie, stood the hundred-foot-tall statue of the hated first Duke of Sutherland, the man responsible for the infamous high clearances when the crofters had been thrown off their lands to make way for sheep. Dornoch, with its famous golf course and thirteenth-century church, was very low on crime. There were no biker gangs in Sutherland. He felt frustrated. Murdo's bland face rose before his eyes. There was something there. The restaurant was outside Strathbane and, therefore, technically on his territory. As he stood there, a mad idea took hold of him.

He went back to the garage and asked if he could rent a motorbike. "Sure," said Sam.

"You couldnae rent me a helmet as well?" asked Hamish.

"Comes wi' the rental."

Hamish began to plan for the evening ahead.

* * *

Shona waved to Dick as he entered the library. He hurried up to her and said, "I'm just going to have another word wi' Hetty. Free for lunch?"

"Aye. Grand."

Shona watched him trot off to where Hetty was seated at her computer. What a nice, steady man, thought Shona. Just the sort of person to make a good partner for Hetty.

She had invited Hetty to a party at her house that evening. Shona had not wanted to issue the invitation, as Hetty had a habit, after a few drinks, of thinking she was irresistible. But Dick might be the answer.

Hetty was scowling at Dick. "What now?"

"I wondered, now that things have calmed down, if you can think of anything about Cyril that might give us a clue as to why he was murdered."

"I don't know," said Hetty shrilly. "I've thought and thought."

"Did he say anything about drugs?"

"He told me stories about drug raids in Strathbane, but nothing in particular."

"Did he mention a restaurant called Seven Steps?"

"He did, I remember. He said he would take me there one evening but he never did."

"Did he ever mention the name Murdo Bentley?"

"No. Now go away. I don't want to think about it any more."

Dick handed over his card. "If you do think of anything, let me know."

He winked at Shona as he left, went out, and waited patiently in his car until she finally emerged for her lunchtime break.

In the café, Dick said, "I'm amazed a bonnie lassie like you isnae married."

"I've actually been engaged twice," said Shona, "but I always got cold feet."

"Why's that?"

"My parents—they're dead now—were always rowing. Then my father started beating my mother. It was awful. Ma once told me that he was lovely when they got married and then it all fell to bits. I'm frightened that would happen to me."

"What you need," said Dick, "is a nice, steady bloke, maybe a wee bit older. How old are you, Shona, if you don't mind me asking?"

"Not a bit. I'm twenty-eight."

That's not bad at all, thought Dick. Twenty-eight's quite mature.

"I'm having a party at my place tonight," said Shona. "Like to come along?"

"Yes, great. What time?"

"Eight o'clock." She took out a card and handed it over. "That's the address. Hetty will be there and maybe she'll give you some bit of information she might have forgotten. Why not bring Mr. Macbeth?"

"I'll ask him," said Dick, "but he's awfy busy."

Dick fretted about the invitation to Hamish all the way

back to Lochdubh. Women always fancied Hamish, he thought gloomily. But if he did not tell Hamish, then he might come across Shona who would say something like, *Sorry you were too busy to come to my party.*

But when he returned to Lochdubh and reluctantly issued the invitation, Hamish only said, "You go. I don't feel like a party." He did not want to get Dick involved in what he planned to do.

As soon as Dick had left that evening, Hamish got into the Land Rover and drove round the end of Lochdubh and into the gloom of the forest on the other side. He drove up into one of the logging trails and parked the Land Rover. Then he settled down to wait.

After a time, he fell asleep, but he had set an alarm clock next to him for midnight. He woke with a start when the alarm went off. He got down from the Land Rover, lifted the motorbike out of the back, and put on the helmet. He was dressed in black: black sweater and black trousers.

He roared off over circuitous back paths until he was clear of the village and then set off in the direction of Strathbane. Just short of the Seven Steps restaurant, he dismounted, donned gloves, and lifted a round heavy rock out of the carrier at the back.

He set off again. When he came level with the plate-glass windows of the restaurant's dining room, he stopped but kept the engine running. The restaurant was in darkness. He hurled the rock straight through the plate-glass windows and sped off, flying along the roads under the blazing stars above.

When he got back to the police station, Dick was in the living room. "Some hooligan's smashed the windows of the Seven Steps restaurant," he said. "We're to get ower there right away."

"Give me a minute to get my uniform on," said Hamish.

Ten minutes later, they set out on the road. "We'll need to see if we can get a look at the tapes from the CCTV cameras," said Hamish. "Probably some drunk. How was the party?"

"Not my thing," said Dick. "I only went in the hope that when Hetty had had a few, she might come up with a bit more information."

"And did she?

"No," said Dick curtly.

Apart from Hetty, the party had consisted of young people of Shona's age. Dick could just about remember when late twenties was not considered young. Shona, looking pretty in a gold sequinned top and a tiny velvet skirt, had settled him on a sofa and then had brought Hetty over to sit beside him. Hetty had been wearing a blouse with a plunging neckline, revealing a black push-up bra underneath. Her face was like a Japanese Noh mask with heavy make-up.

Dick estimated that Hetty had already had quite a bit to drink. Obviously she thought herself irresistible. Shona and her friends were all dancing. When Hetty put a hand on his knee, Dick got up abruptly. He had just seen Shona heading for the kitchen. He was about to go in when he heard a girl say, "Thon policeman doesn't look too happy. Should I ask him for a dance?"

"No," came Shona's voice with dreadful clarity. "Leave the olds to get to know one another. I thought he might be a suitable partner for Hetty."

Dick had walked straight out of the house without saying goodbye, that awful word *olds* ringing in his ears.

Hamish hoped to get to the restaurant before anyone from Strathbane arrived. He now had an excuse to see the CCTV tapes and hoped he could quickly scan back to earlier in the evening to see if there was any face amongst the customers he recognised. It was a long shot. When he had been there with Priscilla everyone looked respectable.

The lights were on in the building when they arrived. A squat, swarthy man with a bald head came out to meet them. "I'm the manager, Bruce Jamieson," he said. "This is awful."

"Do you live on the premises?" asked Hamish.

"Yes, I've got a flat upstairs."

"I'd like a look at your security cameras," said Hamish.

"Come in and I'll show you where they are."

The manager led the way into a small office and switched on the light. "I'll get you the recent tape," he said. He switched on the equipment on a large desk. "You can see we've got monitors for the dining room, the brasserie, and the bar."

"The outside?" asked Hamish.

"Here you go."

Hamish worked the tape backwards. He saw himself roaring up and then speeding off. To his relief, it was not a good shot, more like a blurred image.

"Let me see the tape of who was in the restaurant tonight," said Hamish.

As Hamish slotted in the tape, he could hear approaching sirens. "You'd best go out and talk to them," he said. "I'll go on looking."

He watched the dining room tape for the previous evening. He studied the faces as the camera panned from table to table. The he uttered an exclamation and hit the freeze button. "See anything?" asked Dick.

"Superintendent Daviot and his missus," said Hamish gloomily. He set the tape in motion again.

"What are you doing?" came Jimmy's voice from behind him. "You're supposed to be looking for the man who threw that rock through the window."

"I just wanted to see who was in the restaurant earlier."

"Why?"

Hamish swivelled round but could not see the manager. He said in a low voice, "You know why."

"This is becoming an obsession," snapped Jimmy. "Let me see the tape of the man throwing the rock."

Hamish changed the tapes. Jimmy studied the motorcyclist. "That's a fat lot of good," he said. "This must be an old system. The images aren't very sharp."

"But it's a motorcyclist again," said Hamish. "And Cyril was murdered by a motorbiker. Don't you find that odd?"

"Murderers don't go around throwing rocks."

"So why did he pick this restaurant? There must be a connection."

"Murdo Bentley phoned Daviot and got him out of bed. We're to treat this as priority. A forensic team are on their way. Start tomorrow and check around and see if any bikes have been stolen. I'll take over here."

Hamish slid the tape of the dining room up under his regulation sweater. He held on to his stomach in case it slipped down. "Got indigestion," he said, making for the door.

Dick followed him out.

Before he got in the Land Rover, Hamish scanned the ground nervously for tyre tracks, but the expanse of tarmac outside the restaurant was dry. No tracks.

On the road back, Dick asked, "Why did you steal thon tape? I saw you shoving it up your jumper."

"I want to look at it back at the station in peace and quiet."

In his living room, Hamish slotted in the tape and he and Dick settled back to watch it. "If Daviot's getting free meals, that's certainly going to make life difficult," said Hamish.

"Freeze it!" cried Dick.

"Frozen. What?"

"Thon's the provost and his missus. Michty me!"

"Let's just go in for wild speculation," said Hamish. "Let say Murdo is a criminal. What better security to have than to entertain the great and good of Strathbane wi' freebies?"

"I would ha' thought you were havering afore," said Dick. "But thon manager fair gied me the creeps."

Hamish started the tape again. "Wait a bit," he suddenly said. "I'll go back. Now watch the maître d' going ower to that table. He's a different one from the one in the brasserie."

Dick watched as the maître d' approached a heavyset businessman and a blonde woman at a corner table.

"Freeze!" shouted Dick again. "Thon's Jessie McTavish, one of the most expensive tarts in town."

"Who's the man with her?"

"Don't know."

"Well, watch now," said Hamish, starting up the tape. The maître d' approached the table with a little silver salver. He tilted open the lid. The man nodded. Jessie opened her capacious handbag, and the contents were tipped in.

"Back again and freeze," said Hamish. "Let's see if we can find what's under that salver."

"Can't see," said Dick. "But the man's sliding him a roll of notes."

"Now there's Jessie getting up," said Hamish. "Probably going to the loo. Let's keep watching." At last he said, "Here she comes again. Would you say she had sniffed something or taken something?"

"Can't make it out."

"I'm getting back over there to show this tape to Jimmy. I'll say I took it by accident."

"I'm awfy tired," said Dick.

"Oh, wait here and I'll go myself."

Hoping that Blair hadn't turned up, Hamish headed back to the restaurant.

There was no sign of Blair, but Jimmy was walking up and down outside the taped-off crime scene while the scenes of crime operatives worked the ground.

"Can you leave here?" asked Hamish.

"Why?" asked Jimmy.

"I took a CCTV tape of the dining room by accident."

"You what? You can't do that!"

"It was a mistake," pleaded Hamish. "Could you get in there somehow and say you want to see the tapes again and then give the manager a receipt for this one?"

"Is it that important?"

"I think so."

"Wait there."

Jimmy entered the building by walking against the wall so as not to contaminate the crime scene.

Hamish waited anxiously. Jimmy finally emerged, followed by the manager, Bruce Jamieson, who stared across the car park at Hamish. There was something peculiarly threatening in that stare.

"Got it," said Jimmy curtly. "Have you any booze at that station of yours?"

"Whisky."

"Lead the way."

Dick was asleep on the sofa with the dog on one side and the cat on the other.

"Wakey! Wakey!" yelled Jimmy.

Dick woke with a start and grinned sheepishly. "I'm off to my bed," he said. "I don't need to see it again."

The dog and cat slid off the sofa and disappeared. Hamish fetched a bottle of whisky and two glasses from the kitchen.

He switched on the recorder and slotted in the tape. Jimmy sipped whisky and leaned forward. "Who's the fellow with Jessie?" asked Hamish.

"Car dealer. Johnny Livia. We raided him once. Tip-off he was shipping stolen cars abroad but we couldn't find anything."

Again the maître d' appeared with the little salver. "And that's it?" asked Jimmy. "It isn't enough to raid the place."

"It's enough to ask the maître d' what he gave her. Come on, Jimmy. An iffy car dealer and a well-known tart. I'll do it," said Hamish. "The restaurant is on my beat."

"No, I'll do it but you can come along. I'll meet you outside the restaurant at eleven thirty tomorrow morning when they'll be setting up for lunch. But after us wanting that particular tape, if there is anything going on at the restaurant then they'll make sure it's as clean as a whistle for the next month or so anyway."

✻ ✻ ✻

"Coming?" said Hamish to Dick the following morning.

"Don't feel like it," said Dick. "Don't you sometimes feel worried about getting old?"

"Not yet," said Hamish. "But you could do something for me. Could you check on the computer and see if Murdo owns anything else in Strathbane—pubs or clubs, say?"

"Will do."

"Cheer up. It may never happen. Why are you looking so miserable?"

"I slept badly."

"Nothing to do with that party?"

"No, why should it?" shouted Dick.

"Keep your hair on. I only asked."

While Dick stayed behind to look after the animals and try to find any other businesses that Murdo might own, Hamish set off to meet Jimmy at the restaurant.

It was one of those steel-grey days in the Highlands. No mist, just a canopy of grey cloud overhead and a strange stillness in the landscape. The mountains looked like steel engravings.

A little cloud of midges had managed to get inside the Land Rover. Hamish pulled to the side of the road, took out a spray of insect repellent, and sprayed the inside of the car. Then he realised he had forgotten to open a window and was doubled up with a fit of coughing. He wiped his streaming eyes and set off again.

He parked outside the restaurant and waited until he saw Jimmy driving up before getting out of the Land Rover.

"What did Blair say?" Hamish asked him.

"I didn't tell him. If anyone's been getting free meals or drinks here, Blair's bound to be one of them. Let's get started."

The manager, Bruce Jamieson, had little black eyes which shone with an odd light when Jimmy asked to speak to the maître d' who had been on duty the night before. "That'll be Paolo Gonzales," said Bruce. "Only does evenings."

"Then give us his address," said Jimmy.

"What's this about?"

"Just want a wee word with him. Come on, laddie, get that address."

They waited a quarter of an hour and were about to go in search for the manager when he reappeared and handed them a slip of paper.

"Thanks," said Jimmy. "Come on, Hamish."

Outside, Hamish asked, "Where does he live?"

"Got a wee cottage down the road from here towards Strathbane. Follow me."

As Hamish was about to climb into the Land Rover, he turned and looked at the restaurant. Bruce was standing outside, staring at him.

The cottage turned out to be a low whitewashed building which had once served as a croft house.

Jimmy hammered on the door, and they waited. At last it

was opened by the tall man they recognised from the tape. He had a cadaverous face and pale grey eyes under hooded lids.

"Mr. Gonzales?" asked Jimmy.

"That's me."

Jimmy flashed his warrant card. "Just a wee word. Can we come inside?"

Gonzales shrugged and then stood aside to let them in. The front door led straight into a living-room-*cum*-kitchen. It was sparsely furnished with a round table and four upright chairs. A battered armchair was placed in front of a large television set. A peat fire smoked in the hearth. Gonzales waved an arm to indicate they should sit at the table.

"What's this about?" he asked. He had a faint Spanish accent.

"We've been checking the videotapes at the restaurant," said Jimmy. "We are interested in two of your customers, Johnny Livia and Jessie McTavish. You presented Jessie with something under a silver salver. She put the contents in her handbag and then went to the toilet. What did you give her?"

Gonzales shrugged. "Oh, that? She's got a sweet tooth. The chef makes special marzipan sweets for her."

"Pull the other one," said Jimmy. "Why would she tip sweets into her handbag?"

"Only four of them," said Gonzales blandly, "and they were wrapped in tissue paper."

"Have you ever seen anyone dealing drugs in the restaurant?" asked Hamish.

"I'm shocked you should even ask such a question," said Gonzales. "Seven Steps is a gourmet restaurant. All the best people come, including Superintendent Daviot and his wife."

They persevered with questions but couldn't get anywhere and at last they left.

Outside the cottage, Jimmy's mobile phone rang. He listened and then said, "Right away, sir."

He turned to Hamish. "Daviot's summoned us and he's furious. Let's get it over with."

"What," demanded Daviot as soon as they were shown into his office, "do you mean by questioning a respectable waiter from the best restaurant in the Highlands and implying they were dealing drugs?"

Jimmy patiently told him about the tape.

"You should have come to me or Mr. Blair first," raged Daviot. "I eat there myself and I have never seen anything untoward."

"I was there myself, sir, last night in the brasserie with Miss Halburton-Smythe," said Hamish. "We were offered a free meal. That in itself is suspicious."

Daviot turned pink. "What is so suspicious about a generous offer like that?"

"Restaurants or bars which offer coppers freebies are often trying to get favours. I mean, if someone as eminent as yourself were to be offered a free meal, of course you would turn it down."

Suddenly it seemed as if Daviot could not wait to be rid of them.

"So our master and chief *was* taking freebies," said Hamish as they walked down the stairs.

"Think so?"

"Aye, and he'll spread the word around the lodge. I think Murdo will find that his best customers suddenly don't want any presents at all."

"What about going to see Jessie?"

"I've still got Cyril's murder to solve. You can go your-self."

Hamish downloaded Jessie's address from a police computer. She had only been charged once, and that had been for drunk and disorderly. Nothing about drugs.

He met Constable Annie Williams on the road out. He showed her Jessie's address. "Do you know where this is?"

"Aye, went on a raid there once. It's a brothel. Just before you leave Strathbane on the Oban road, turn left down Glebe Street and it's the villa at the end. Fancy dinner tonight?"

Hamish had once had a one-night stand with Annie, only to find out the next day that she was married. "Things to do, people to see," he said, brushing past her.

* * *

He found the villa, wondering why the brothel had not been closed down, and then realised whoever ran it was probably paying the police to be left alone.

He rang the bell. The door was opened by a small, grey-haired, sour-looking woman. Her face hardened when she saw him. "I'm not paying any mair," she said.

Hamish hesitated for a moment. Should he demand to know which corrupt police or policemen were demanding money to leave her alone? Then he thought of the endless reports and investigations. Another time, he decided.

Aloud, he said, "I just wanted a wee word wi' Jessie McTavish."

"She's left. Gone tae live wi' a car salesman."

Hamish touched his cap, said, "Thank you," and turned to go.

"Wait!" she called. "You seem like a nice lad. Like a bit o' something?"

"Forget it." Hamish got into the Land Rover and drove off. Now for Johnny Livia. He stopped at the end of the street and fished out a battered copy of the Highlands and Islands telephone book. There was a private address for Johnny Livia on the other side of Strathbane.

Johnny Livia's home turned out to be fake Georgian. It had once been a Victorian villa, but he had put a pillared entrance on the front. There was a short drive leading to the house, lined on either side with laurel bushes.

Hamish rang the bell, which tinkled out a chorus of "Scotland the Brave." The door was jerked open and Jessie

McTavish glared up at him. Her bleached hair was tousled, and she was wrapped in a silk dressing gown.

"Whit now?" she demanded. "I ain't done nothing."

"Just a talk," said Hamish.

"Go away!"

"I can stand out here and shout," said Hamish. He bellowed, "I want to ask you about drugs!"

"Come in, for God's sake," said Jessie.

The living room into which she led him looked as if it had been little used. It was crammed with reproduction Louis Quinze furniture, gilt-framed mirrors, and a white-leather-padded bar.

"I have naethin' tae dae wi' drugs," said Jessie fishing in the pocket of her dressing gown and producing a packet of cigarettes.

"I just wanted to ask you what the maître d' gave you last night when he brought that small silver salver over to your table?"

A phone beside Jessie on a small table rang shrilly. She picked it up and listened and then said, "Aye, right," and rang off.

"You was asking about last night?" said Jessie. She lit a cigarette and puffed a cloud of smoke in Hamish's direction. "That was some sweeties I'm partial to."

"Why put them in your handbag and go to the toilet?"

"I had tae pee. Right? Now if that's all you want…"

"I'll be watching you from now on," said Hamish.

She rose to escort him to the door. Just as he was going

to leave, Hamish turned suddenly and thrust up a sleeve of her dressing gown.

"Those are track marks, Jessie."

"I'm clean!"

"Those are fresh. You are playing a dangerous game, whatever you've got yourself into."

Her eyes blazed with anger. "They'll sort you out, copper. I've got powerful friends."

"I'll be back with a search warrant."

Jessie slammed the door on him. Once inside, she rushed to the phone, dialled a number, and spoke rapidly.

Hamish phoned Jimmy and reported on his visit. "I can't see us getting a search warrant because some brass nail has fresh tracks on her arms," said Jimmy. "If we got search warrants for every prostitute in Strathbane wi' track marks, we'd never get through the work. Get back over to Sandybeach and search around again."

When Hamish returned to the police station, Dick said, "Nothing on Murdo, but that manager owns a club in Strathbane."

"Now, that's odd," said Hamish. "If he owns a club in Strathbane, what's he doing managing a restaurant? What's the club called?"

"Queen Draggie."

"A drag club! I suppose you can find everything in Strathbane if you lift enough stones. We'll try it later. I've got to go back up to Sandybeach."

"I'll keep on looking," said Dick, hoping for a lazy day.

"All right. I'll leave you to look after Sonsie and Lugs."

Hamish called in at the Tommel Castle Hotel, where he found Priscilla in the gift shop. He told her what he had found out so far.

"I don't like this," said Priscilla. "I think you might be in danger."

"If they killed Cyril, they won't want to bump off another policeman. I might try visiting that drag club."

"I'll come with you."

"It might be dangerous."

"We could just suss out the place."

"All right. I'll pick you up at nine o'clock this evening. Might take Dick as well. The very sight of us might shake something loose."

Hamish felt he had spent a wasted day by the time he returned to the police station. Dick looked sulky at the idea of the visit to the drag club.

They got dressed in smart casual clothes and collected Priscilla from the Tommel Castle Hotel. She was wearing a sequinned top over tight black velvet trousers. She wrapped herself in a scarlet mohair stole.

"We'll take my car," she said.

"No, we'd better use Dick's old banger. This club is down at the docks and your Mercedes might get stolen," said Hamish.

As they drove off through the darkness of the Highlands and then looked down on the orange sodium glow that was Strathbane, Hamish said, "Every time I approach the place, I wonder that such a hell can exist in the beauty of the Highlands."

Dick at the wheel made his way to the docks, now largely in rusting ruins. Facing the oily waterfront where a discarded sofa bobbed on the water, the neon sign above the club flashed on and off in the darkness.

The entry fee was ten pounds each. A man dressed as a bunny girl led them to a table. Hamish looked around. The club seemed to be ignoring the smoking ban. There was a small stage where a man in drag was performing "Hello Dolly" in a thick Glasgow accent.

"None of them even looks like a woman," said Priscilla as another drag queen came on the stage. He was squat and hairy.

"Should have at least shaved his chest," said Dick.

The audience was mostly made up of young people, the feral youth of Strathbane.

The "bunny girl" approached their table carrying a bottle of champagne in an ice bucket. "On the hoose, darlings," she said.

"No freebies," said Hamish curtly. "Take it away and bring us…?"

"Beer," said Dick.

"Lager," said Priscilla.

"And I'll have a tonic water," said Hamish.

He shrugged and teetered off on his stilettos.

"We've been spotted," said Hamish. "If there's any drug dealing going on, they'll wait until we leave."

"Got to go to the ladies' room," said Priscilla. She edged her way through the tables to where a sign for the toilets was lit up over a side door.

Three girls were huddled in a corner. She heard one say in a low voice, "We cannae get anything the night."

Priscilla had sharp ears. She heard another one whisper, "If ye want anything, you're to go out the back door."

Priscilla quickly pretended to repair her make-up and hurried back to their table.

"The drugs are being dealt at the back door," she said.

"I don't want anyone to see me making a phone call," said Hamish.

Their drinks arrived. "That'll be thirty-five quid," said the waitress.

"That's too much," said Hamish.

"Pay it or get out."

"I've got money in the car," said Hamish. "I'll be right back. Give me the keys, Dick."

He hurriedly left the club. Outside, he got into Dick's car, bent down as if looking for something, and made a call to Jimmy. "I'm at the Queen Draggie club. They're dealing drugs at the back door. Raid the bloody place."

He returned to the club where the "bunny girl" was hovering beside their table, took out his wallet, and paid him. He shoved the money in his bra and went off.

After twenty minutes, when Hamish was just beginning to think the police would never arrive, he heard a loud altercation and then the club seemed to be full of police. People were scrambling to get out and finding their way blocked.

"Aren't we going to join in?" asked Dick.

"There are enough of them. It wouldn't be a good idea to leave Priscilla."

The music had died. They watched as the customers were searched. Police were dropping packets of pills and little glassine envelopes into forensic bags.

At last, Jimmy came up to them. "Good work, Hamish. What put you on to it?"

"The manager of the Seven Steps owns this club. What is Murdo Bentley doing with a manager who owns a club that deals drugs? And why is Bruce working as a manager when he owns a club?"

"We'll be looking into that. Type up a statement and send it over."

On the road home, Hamish said happily, "Well, that's got the ball rolling. What if Cyril was the tip-off?"

"Could ha' been," said Dick. "But why bump him off?"

"Maybe he was caught selling their drugs on the side," said Hamish. "Like to come in for a nightcap, Priscilla?"

"No thanks. Just drop me off at the hotel."

Hamish uncurled himself from the backseat of Dick's little car when they arrived at the police station. The large flap on the station door banged open and Lugs erupted out, barking shrilly. He was followed by Sonsie, whose fur was raised and whose eyes were blazing.

"There, now," said Hamish. "What's up?"

Lugs ran to the front garden and continued barking.

Dick and Hamish opened the little side gate to the garden. Hamish took out a torch and shone it.

The body of Jessie McTavish lay on the grass, her dead eyes staring up at the Sutherland sky.

Chapter Five

Every harlot was a virgin once.

—*William Blake*

Hamish sat hunched at the kitchen table during that long night. He had answered question after question. First there was Blair, shouting and bullying and stopping just short of accusing him of the murder. Then Jimmy and Detective Andy McNab with more questions.

Hamish explained over and over again that he had questioned her about what she had received from the maître d' in the restaurant. She had insisted it was sweets. That was all. He had not seen her since. He had been up around Sandybeach questioning people who lived on the road there, and he had gone to the drag club.

Then they would switch from grilling him and turn their attention to Dick.

At last Daviot arrived on the scene and sent the detectives outside. He sat down heavily opposite Hamish and Dick and said wearily, "This is a bad, bad business, but you're in the clear. Forensics and the pathologist have found that she was killed some time earlier with a savage blow to the head. The body was then driven to Lochdubh and thrust over the hedge into your front garden. There are breaks in the hedge showing where the body caught parts of it before being shoved in."

"It's all tied up to drugs somehow. How did the raid on the club go?" asked Hamish.

"Drugs were found in the manager's office. Bruce Jamieson has been arrested."

"And what did Murdo Bentley say about his restaurant manager being a drug peddler?"

"He is deeply shocked. He swears he was unaware that Jamieson even owned a club."

"Oh, sir, that's hard to believe."

"Murdo Bentley has long been an outstanding member of the community. He contributes regularly to various charities, including the police widows' and orphans' pension fund. Good heavens, Macbeth, he even had a new wing of Strathbane hospital built."

"What about Paolo Gonzales, the maître d'? Does he have any sort of record?"

"Nothing at all. Not even a parking ticket."

"And Johnny Livia, the car dealer she was living with?"

"Alibied up to the hilt. Down at a sales conference in Glasgow."

"But Murdo Bentley will surely be watched and investigated from now on."

Daviot rose to his feet. "Leave it with me."

Which means, thought Hamish savagely as the kitchen door closed behind the superintendent, that nothing will be done at all.

In Glasgow, news presenter Elspeth Grant heard about the body in Hamish's garden. She wondered if she would be sent there to report because of her friendship with Hamish. But as she studied film of the scene on the waterfront at Lochdubh, she suddenly saw Hamish talking to Priscilla. Elspeth had been briefly engaged to Hamish but had broken it off because she had found he was spending time with Priscilla. She was suddenly determined not to go, even if ordered to do so.

"I really have to get back to my job in London, Hamish," Priscilla said as they stood outside the station watching Daviot give a press conference.

"I think I'll go fishing," said Hamish, "and by the time I get back, with any luck the press will have gone."

"Why on earth did they dump her body in your garden?" asked Priscilla. "I mean, the murder of a prostitute would only merit a few lines in the press. But the body of a prostitute in a policeman's garden is big news."

"It's a warning to me," said Hamish. "They want me to know they are all-powerful and that I could be next."

"Just be careful," said Priscilla.

"Would you miss me if I were dead?" asked Hamish.

"Really, Hamish!" said Priscilla. "It's not like you to stoop to emotional blackmail. Bye."

Hamish scowled after her. "Bitch," he muttered.

"Who's a bitch?" asked a voice behind him.

Hamish swung round and found Angela Brodie behind him.

"Life in general," said Hamish. "How are things?"

"Not exactly pleasant. I spent an awful lot of money on a gown for the awards ceremony and my husband is sulking. It's *my* money, I told him."

"Doesn't sound at all like your man. How much did you pay?"

"Nearly two thousand pounds."

"Michty me! Is it gold-plated?"

"No, I got it made in Inverness."

"I know Inverness is a boomtown these days, but I didn't think it would have a place with that sort of price."

"It's called Modes, and you can buy or get something made. The place I first thought of didn't have much."

"I didn't know you and Dr. Brodie ever quarrelled about anything."

"We hardly ever do. Could you have a word with him, Hamish? I've got a feeling it's something other than money."

"Is he in the surgery?"

"He's at home at the moment. I don't know what's come

over him. I've never known him to be mean about money before."

"I'll see what I can do."

Hamish's insatiable highland curiosity was pricked. He found Dr. Brodie in his kitchen, drinking coffee and reading a newspaper.

"What's brought you?" asked Dr. Brodie. "Coffee?"

"No thanks."

"It's not Angela's. I got a flask from Patel. He's started to sell hot coffee."

"Well, in that case..." Hamish poured a mug of coffee and sat down at the table.

"It's like this," he said. "Your wife is right upset because you've turned nasty about her dress."

"Did she tell you how much it cost?"

"Aye. But she's fair excited about this award."

"Did she tell you she's got a new publisher for this detective story?"

"No. She did tell me she'd written it under another name."

"Her editor was up here a while back," said the doctor moodily.

"So?"

"He looks like Tom Cruise. They went off together to Strathbane for lunch and she didn't come back until the evening. She was all giggles. His name is Charles Davenport. Twice during the night since then, she's said 'Charles' in her sleep. Then she shot off to pay a fortune for this wretched dress."

"Why didn't you tell her you were jealous?"

"Me! Jealous?"

"Yes. You."

"I was just angry that she was making a damn fool of herself."

"Come on, man. This is Angela's big moment and you're spoiling it for her."

Dr. Brodie stared down into his coffee mug. "She's a very attractive woman."

Hamish thought of Angela with her mild pleasant face and wispy hair. Wish someone could love me as blindly as that, he thought.

"Look," said Dr. Brodie, "you stood in for me before. Could you escort her?"

"Me? Why?"

"If I go, I'll spoil her evening by being rude to that popinjay, Davenport. I know I will."

"Where is it, again?"

"Yon restaurant—Seven Steps."

"I'd be glad to," said Hamish quickly. "But what will you tell her?"

"I'll pretend to be ill. On a Monday morning, my surgery is full of folk pretending to be ill. I can join the club."

Angela met Hamish on the waterfront as he strolled back to the police station. "Well?" she demanded.

"Your man is jealous."

"What!"

"You went off for a long, long lunch wi' a gorgeous-looking editor."

"Oh, the dear man!"

"I think you'll find he's all right now."

Angela stood on tiptoe and kissed Hamish on the cheek. "Thanks for everything."

"Did you see that?" demanded Nessie Currie. "That Hamish Macbeth just can't leave the women alone."

"Alone," echoed her sister as the twins went off arm in arm to Patel's shop to spread the gossip.

Hamish went back to the police station to try to think what he could possibly do about Murdo Bentley. He daren't approach the man for fear of Daviot hearing about it.

Dick had left him a note on the kitchen table. "Gone up to Sandybeach to see if there might be anything we missed."

Wondering why the usually lazy Dick had decided to go and do some police work on his own initiative, Hamish thought it was time he took some action himself.

He put the dog and cat in the Land Rover and set off on the Strathbane road.

Dick was not going to Sandybeach but to the library in Braikie. He felt that if Shona would only smile at him, it would take the dreadful memory of that *olds* remark away.

A good part of his mind told him he was behaving like a lovesick teenager, but the rest craved seeing her again.

When he entered the library, he could hear Shona's voice coming from the children's section. He was just heading in that direction when a voice hailed him. "Mr. Fraser?"

He swung round. Hetty stood there smiling at him. "Looking for me?"

She had lipstick on her teeth.

"Aye," said Dick. He could just hear Shona saying, "And then they lived happily ever after," and the chatter of children's voices. "I wondered if you had remembered anything?" he said.

She shook her head.

"Did he ever talk about his ambitions? Was he always going to be a policeman?"

Hetty looked at her watch. "I was just about to go for lunch. Why don't we go together?"

"Oh, all right," said Dick, his heart plummeting down into his regulation boots.

A wave of small children swept past, followed by Shona. "We were just about to go for lunch," said Dick quickly. "Would you care to join us?"

"Not possible," said Hetty. "You've got that cataloguing to do. I'll get my coat."

"It'll need to be another time," said Shona. She giggled. "Hetty wants you all to herself."

"I'm only interviewing her as part o' my duties," said Dick.

Shona grinned. "I think our Hetty is sweet on you."

Hetty came hurrying back before Dick could reply. She hooked her arm around Dick's arm and gave him what she considered her best winsome smile.

Hetty chose the nearest pub, The Cameron, for lunch. It had been Scottishified by some brewery with plastic claymores on the wall and tartan carpet on the floor. Hetty ordered something called a Highland Slammer to drink. It came in a tall glass with two paper umbrellas. Dick had an orange juice and looked at the menu.

Hetty ordered Rabbie Burns broth to start followed by Prince Charlie's Angus steak and chips. Then she asked for the wine list and chose a bottle of Merlot.

Dick ordered Granny's Highland Haggis, the cheapest thing on the menu, and hoped he could get the price of the meal back on expenses.

"So," said Dick, "did Cyril say anything about his plans for the future? I mean, had he ambitions to be a detective?"

"No, he didn't like them at Strathbane. Said they were a bunch of sheep shaggers." Hetty laughed uproariously and Dick winced. "He said he was going to be rich and travel."

"How did he plan to get the money to do that?"

"He said something about a change of career, but that was all."

Hetty finished her Highland Slammer and started on the wine. "He did love me, you know," she said, leaning across the table and looking into Dick's eyes.

"You've got lipstick on your teeth," said Dick.

She scowled at him and scrubbed her teeth with her napkin.

"Excuse me!" Dick got to his feet and hurried to the men's room. He phoned Hamish.

"Could you phone me back in five minutes and order me out on a job?" pleaded Dick.

"Will do. What's up?"

"Tell you later."

Dick spent a few minutes washing his hands before returning to the table. Hetty was becoming tipsy. She waggled a finger at him. "I know what you're after."

Dick's phone rang. He answered it and said, "Right away, sir."

When he rang off, he said to Hetty, "Got a job. I'll square this before I go."

He rushed up to the bar and paid the bill. Hetty's voice followed him as he left the restaurant. "When will I see you again?"

As Dick left he saw Shona leaving the library. He felt he had made enough of a fool of himself for one day and was about to get into his car when she hailed him. "Hullo, Dick. Where's Hetty?"

"She's in the pub. I've been called out on a job."

"What a pity. You and Hetty seem to be getting on well."

"My only interest in Hetty," said Dick, "is to see if she can remember anything important about Cyril. How can you stand the woman?"

"Oh, Hetty's all right. I'm a bit sorry for her. She's lonely."

"I wonder why?" said Dick acidly.

She gave him a startled look, and Dick blushed. "Sorry to sound so cross," he said. "But Hetty was getting drunk and I got fed up. I would rather have had lunch with you."

"Maybe another time," said Shona.

Dick sadly watched her walk away.

Hamish parked the Land Rover off the road under a stand of birch trees some distance from where Paolo Gonzales lived. He was out of uniform, dressed again in black trousers and a sweater with a black woollen hat pulled down over his red hair. He let the dog and cat run around the moorland for a bit before shutting them up in the Land Rover.

The day had turned grey with a fine mist drifting across the landscape. Hamish did not know what he expected to see. Johnny Livia had been pulled in for questioning about the murder of Jessie McTavish, but Hamish was sure the man would simply repeat his cast-iron alibi. He felt he could not spend another day idle. Perhaps if he covertly watched Paolo's cottage, he might learn something.

He approached the cottage by a circuitous route. He noticed that although the day was quite chilly, there was no smoke rising from the chimney, nor was there any car outside. It was possible that the man was at the restaurant.

There was no point in watching an empty house. Hamish had a sudden longing to get inside the cottage to see if he could find anything incriminating. He was risking his job if he went in there without a search warrant. He looked around at the empty landscape and felt in his pocket for his skeleton keys.

He cautiously approached the door. He decided to try the handle before picking the lock. The handle turned and the door swung open. Hamish went inside. If caught, he could always say he had smelt gas.

Not only was the living-room-*cum*-kitchen deserted, but there were signs of hasty packing. The television had gone along with the plates, pots, and pans.

A large discarded packing case with a split in its side lay on the floor.

Hamish suddenly heard the sound of a vehicle arriving. He darted out of the unlocked back door. There was no garden, only heather and gorse. Hamish crouched down behind a gorse bush.

He could hear sounds of activity from inside. He crept up and looked through the small window at the back. Two men he did not recognise were hard at work. One was washing the floor with bleach while the other was wiping all the surfaces.

Hamish wriggled away as far as he could and then stood up and ran. When he thought he was a far enough distance away, he phoned Jimmy. He told him what he had seen. "They're covering up some crime," he said.

"Sit tight," said Jimmy. "I'll be over right away."

Hamish returned to his post behind the gorse bush. He

fretted that the men would be long gone before Jimmy arrived, but finally heaved a sigh of relief when he heard cars arriving.

He hurried round to the front of the house in time to hear one of the men saying, "We were just cleaning up. This is a rented cottage. Paolo's gone back to Spain."

"You pair stay outside," barked Jimmy. "Names?"

"I'm Andy Campbell and this is my brither, Davy."

Jimmy turned to Hamish. "Get a suit and follow me in."

Hamish borrowed a forensic suit from one of the policemen, covered his boots, and joined Jimmy inside the cottage.

"Keep ower by the door, Hamish," said Jimmy. "A forensic team's on its road."

"I guess the bedroom's upstairs," said Hamish. "I wish we could take a look at it."

"Well, we can't until forensics have done their work. We'll get this pair down to headquarters for questioning."

It turned out to be a long day. The brothers did odd jobs for a company called Highland Rentals. Neither of them had a record. The initial forensic report said that strong bleach had been poured over the stone kitchen floor, and so far there was no sign of anything sinister. Paolo Gonzales had relatives in Malaga, and a check at Inverness airport showed he had taken a morning flight to Malaga the day before. The brothers were released.

"Waste o' time," said Jimmy. "Go home, Hamish."

* * *

Hamish drove out on the road to Lochdubh and stopped to
let Sonsie and Lugs out for a run in the heather. He stared up
at the starry sky and thought hard. There were still, he felt
sure, a whole lot of questions that hadn't been asked. Who,
for example, owned Highland Rentals? Their offices were in
Strathbane. If he called on them in the morning, he would
get a rocket from Strathbane for poaching on their territory.

Then he would like to see the CCTV shots of who exactly got on the Malaga plane. He suddenly decided to risk
the wrath of the Inverness police and call at the airport in
the morning. He could ask Inverness police to do it but they
didn't know what Paolo looked like and he did. And it would
mean waiting to try to find a photograph—and Hamish had
a feeling that all photographs of the maître d' might have
disappeared.

Jimmy phoned when he got back to the station. "Highland
Rentals seems as clean as a whistle," he said.

"Who owns it?"

"A woman called Beryl Shuttleworth. Actually she lives
near your village. Got a place out past the Tommel Castle
Hotel. Called The Firs."

"I know that. I thought old Mr. Anstruther lived there."

"You're not checking on the folk on your beat. He died
a month ago, and his daughter sold it to the Shuttleworth
woman."

"I don't remember any funeral," said Hamish, who knew
that local funerals were a big event.

"He was originally from Somerset, and that's where the daughter took him to be buried."

"I might call on her."

"Don't! She's a friend o' Daviot's missus."

"Is all investigation to be hampered because of Daviot's friends?"

"If you want to keep your station, you'll go carefully."

"Did anyone think to check the CCTV cameras at Inverness airport to see if Gonzales really left?"

"Wait a bit...Some report's just coming in."

Hamish waited, hearing exclamations and questions and then Blair's voice raging, "Get thon two back in here. Released? Which damn numpty let them oot?"

At last Jimmy came on the phone. "Bad news, Hamish."

Hamish sighed. "It wasnae Gonzales who got on that plane with his passport?"

"That's it," said Jimmy. "And the brothers, Andy and Davy Campbell, were released."

"So what does the substitute look like? Anyone you know?"

"Same height, roughly the same features, but definitely not Gonzales."

"Don't you see that all roads lead back to Murdo Bentley?"

"Get off that phone!" howled Blair's voice in the background, and Hamish was cut off.

Hamish went into the living room. "Dick, did you know about a newcomer to the area, Beryl Shuttleworth?"

"Oh, her. Aye. I called on her to say hullo about a month ago. Nice lady."

"Why didn't you tell me about her?"

"Didn't seem important. You turned over the job of calling on the locals to me. What's the interest in her?"

Hamish told him about the disappearance of Gonzales. "I'll go and see her," he said.

"Want me to come?"

"No. Are you absolutely sure that Hetty doesn't know anything? Might be an idea to keep after her."

Dick repressed a shudder. Then he had an idea. "Instead of questioning Hetty again," he said, "I could ask that other librarian, Shona, if Hetty said anything to her."

"Good idea."

Dick brightened. "Do you mind if I don't take Sonsie and Lugs with me?"

"No, it's all right. They can come with me."

Followed by his pets, Hamish walked up to the manse. The minister's wife, Mrs. Wellington, was in her gloomy kitchen, taking a tray of scones out of the Raeburn cooker.

"Come in," she said. "What do you want? Oh, leave those terrifying beasts of yours outside."

Hamish walked out of the kitchen. "Stay!" he ordered.

When he went back in, Mrs. Wellington boomed, "A few centuries ago they would have burnt you as a warlock. It's unnatural for a cat to obey orders."

Every time he saw Mrs. Wellington, Hamish felt a stab

of pity for the mild-mannered minister. His wife was so domineering, so *tweedy*, with her round figure and bulldog face.

"What do you want?" she demanded.

"What sort of person is Beryl Shuttleworth?"

"Mrs. Shuttleworth to you. I don't hold with all this touchy-feely business of calling folk by their first names."

"Okay, Mrs. Shuttleworth."

"Nice lady. Comes to the kirk on Sunday which is more than you can say for a lot of the godless in this village."

"What does Mr. Shuttleworth do?"

"She's a widow. Why are you so interested?"

"I like to call on newcomers to the area."

"She's got an office in Strathbane."

Hamish inwardly cursed. He had forgotten that. And he should have realised that the Inverness police would check at the airport to see if Gonzales really got on the plane.

He looked hopefully at the coffee percolator. Mrs. Wellington said, "No coffee for you. I do not encourage mooching."

Hamish walked down the brae from the manse with the dog and cat at his heels. Dark clouds were streaming in from the west. Choppy waves raced over the surface of the loch. He had not heard the weather forecast but he was sure Sutherland was about to release one of its monumental gales on the landscape.

At the police station, he put his pets in the back of the Land Rover and drove off out of the village. He decided there might just be a chance of getting a break in the—now two—murder cases.

The Firs was a Scottish Georgian villa, standing on a rise, with a view down to the loch. It was made of sandstone and covered in ivy. The iron gates stood open. Hamish could not remember them ever being closed. There was a short twisting drive bordered by rhododendron bushes opening out into a circular gravelled area in front of the house. To one side of the house was a shaggy lawn with two stands of pampas grass.

Hamish got down from the Land Rover. He walked to one of the front windows and looked in. A woman was sitting reading a newspaper. He backed away hurriedly, went to the door, and rang the bell.

He could hear the click of high heels, and then the door opened.

"Mrs. Shuttleworth?" asked Hamish.

"If it's about Andy and Davy Campbell, I have already spoken to the police."

"Just a few more questions. I am Police Sergeant Hamish Macbeth."

"I suppose you'd better come in."

As he followed her trim figure, Hamish wondered what sort of woman wore a power suit to sit at the fire and read a newspaper.

She sat down in an armchair by the fire and indicated

that Hamish should sit in an armchair opposite. Hamish removed his cap and put it on his knees.

Beryl Shuttleworth was a woman he guessed to be in her late forties. She had black hair worn in a French pleat. Her skin was good. She had a long thin nose and hooded eyes, giving her face a medieval look.

Hamish looked around the room. Apart from the comfortable armchairs and the heavy brocaded curtains at the long windows, it looked as if it had been furnished by Ikea. There was a modern wooden desk by the window with an Apple computer on top. Wooden shelves held various greenhouse plants and ornaments. There was a long plain wooden coffee table. In one corner was a very large flat-screen television.

"Are you going to sit there gawping?" demanded Beryl.

"Sorry," said Hamish. "About the Campbell brothers, how did you come to employ them?"

"I advertised for a couple of odd-job men to do gardening work on my various properties as well as moving furniture and things like that."

"Did you check their references?"

"I didn't ask for any. These days it's hard to get labour."

"Did they usually clean places for you?"

"No, I have maids to do that. Look, I have already been asked all these questions and I don't see why I should have to waste time answering them again."

Hamish smiled at her, a smile that lit up his thin face. "Persevering police like me can be a pain in the bum."

She gave a reluctant laugh. "It was some detective called Blair. He ranted and raved at me."

"Do you know Mr. Murdo Bentley?"

"Of course. I go to his restaurant quite often."

"Do you know if he had ever employed the Campbell brothers before?"

"Mr. Bentley is not a close friend of mine. The Campbell brothers were odd-job men. They were not exclusive to me. Would you like some coffee?"

"Yes, please."

Hamish watched her as she left the room. No one would ever call Beryl beautiful, but she exuded a strong aura of sensuality. He looked longingly at the computer. He sometimes wished he could forge search warrants. Then his sharp eyes noticed a framed photograph on her desk. It had been placed facedown. Why?

He eased himself to his feet, darted across to the desk, and was just reaching out to lift the photo when he heard the clink of china as Beryl returned. Hamish sat down again hurriedly.

"Here we are." She placed a tray on the coffee table. "Milk and sugar?"

"Just black, thank you."

"So Mr. Macbeth…"

"Hamish, please."

"Very well. Hamish, what do you do when you are not hunting down villains?"

"I've got a bit of a croft at the back of the police station. I keep sheep and some hens."

"And are you happy with your life?"

"Most of the time. But not when I am investigating a murder like this."

She was just in the act of pouring herself a cup of coffee. Her hand shook, and some coffee spilled over into the saucer.

Her eyes under their hooded lids were black, the kind of eyes that do not show any expression.

"Murder? But I thought you were trying to find a missing man and also to find out what the Campbell brothers were doing cleaning up his cottage. As I told Mr. Blair, I did not order them to do so."

Hamish told her that Gonzales was still missing and that someone else had used his passport to leave the country.

She took a tissue out of a box and mopped up the spilled coffee from her saucer.

"It's all a mystery to me," she said. "But I am sure that when you find Andy and Davy Campbell, all will be explained."

Hamish noticed that the thought of the brothers being found did not seem to make her nervous.

"Why did you move to an isolated spot like this?" he asked. "It can get a bit grim in the winter."

"I was brought up in a cottage on the Yorkshire moors. I like the countryside."

Hamish fished out one of his cards and handed it over. "If you do hear anything, let me know."

He rose to his feet. There was a landscape painting

hanging over the desk. He walked over and studied it. He planned to say something like, *Did I knock this over?* and lift the photograph. But she had come up behind him and put an arm around his waist.

"I've enjoyed our visit," said Beryl, urging him towards the door. "But I do have work to do."

She gave him a push. "Goodbye, Hamish Macbeth."

Outside, he sat in the Land Rover and wondered if he was placing too much importance on that photograph.

He decided to send Dick in plainclothes down to her office in Strathbane. He could collect a brochure, find out where the cottages to rent were, and then see what sort of people rented them.

The gale was howling straight in from the Atlantic, over the Gulf Stream, bringing a false warmth of spring. Hamish stood by the Land Rover, remembering as a child how he had cartwheeled before the wind. He wondered if he could still do it. The wind was at his back. He suddenly took off down the drive, performed five cartwheels, and returned to the Land Rover in triumph. Beryl watched him through the window. The man's nothing but a fool, she thought, and picked up the phone.

Dick was having lunch with Shona. Outside the café, the wind howled and screamed, sending rubbish flying along the street.

"So you want me to spy on Hetty?" Shona was asking.

"Not spy, exactly. Encourage her to talk about Cyril. He seemed to think he was going to come into money."

"I'll try. But Hetty treats me a bit like an underling, not as a friend. They must have searched Cyril's lodgings in Strathbane. Didn't they find anything?"

Dick took out his iPad and flicked through his notes. "No. Nothing there."

"But you think Cyril was into something crooked?"

"Must have been to get murdered so brutally."

"I know," said Shona. "I'll suggest to Hetty that we have a drink after work. She can't resist the offer of a drink."

"That's very good of you." Dick gazed into her eyes, and then sharply reminded himself of the age difference.

Shona glanced at her watch and gave an exclamation. "I'd better get back." Dick paid the bill and escorted her outside. The wind seized his cap and sent it flying off down the street. By the time he retrieved it and turned around, Shona had disappeared into the library.

Chapter Six

But I am not so think as you drunk I am.

—J. C. Squire

In the following weeks, Hamish began to feel they would never get anywhere.

Before, he had experienced an intuitive feeling that his life might be in danger, but now, even that feeling had gone. He had forgotten all about the awards ceremony until reminded by a nervous Angela, saying her husband was ill and he would have to escort her.

Delighted to have an opportunity of seeing the inside of Seven Steps again, Hamish gladly agreed.

To his surprise, Angela had hired a white Mercedes limousine and driver to take them there. Her usually wispy hair had been firmly rolled and set into ridged curls and waves. Her face was a mask of make-up, and her frightened eyes shone out of circles of black eyeliner.

She was wearing a tailored blue silk evening coat over a long blue sequined gown. "Aren't you going to be cold?" asked Hamish.

"No. We're to make an entrance up the red carpet and be photographed. The car's warm and the restaurant will be warm. You'd better leave your coat in the car."

Photographers were massed outside the restaurant. They were all quite young, and Hamish did not recognise any of them. He cynically wondered if the sofa company had hired them for the evening from some local camera society.

They shouted, "Turn this way, T. J.," and Angela shot delighted smiles all round.

"Who's T. J.?" asked Hamish.

"I forgot to tell you. That's my new writing name, T. J. Leverage."

Angela's new editor came forward to meet them. "This is Charles Davenport," said Angela. "Charles, my husband couldn't make it. This is Hamish Macbeth."

Charles ignored Hamish. "Now, you're about to be welcomed by Strathbane Television. You just say a few words. It's being pre-recorded. It goes out next Monday."

A thin anorexic woman held out a microphone. "What do you think of the event, T. J.?"

"It seems very nice," said Angela.

The presenter put her hand over the microphone and glared at Angela. "We'll do that again. You are to say that it's all very exciting."

Angela did as ordered but in a weak, small voice. "Now

you go to the green room with me," said Charles. "They're going to do a full interview with you."

At a half-screened-off area, a writer with a long white beard was saying how much the hills and heather had inspired him.

"Who is going to interview Angela?" asked Hamish.

"The sofa company director's missus, Joan Bramston."

"What's that?" asked Angela.

"Nothing important," said Hamish quickly. He did not want to depress Angela by telling her she was about to be interviewed by some businessman's wife who wanted her moment of glory.

At last Angela was ushered forward. She found herself facing a well-upholstered woman who was encased in gold sequins. She had a fat, truculent face.

The interview began. "What made you change your writing?" asked Joan. "Did you decide to cash in on a more popular market?"

"No, I…"

"A lot of writers do that. Don't you think it is immoral to glorify murder?"

"No," replied Angela and then was at a loss for words.

At last, she was released after several more questions, feeling as if she had been mugged.

"Now we go through to the dining room," said Charles.

"Wait a bit," said Hamish. "Angela, there are lassies over there doing make-up. Might be an idea to let them do a professional job."

Demoralised, Angela agreed. The transformation was quick and successful. Her face had been expertly made up and her rigid hairstyle loosened.

They made their way to the dining room. Their table was at the very back of the room. Their dining companions introduced themselves. Angela promptly forgot all their names in her nervousness. But as the conversation started, she found she was the only writer at the table apart from a surly young man in a polo-neck sweater who said he wrote children's stories. The other three men turned out to be shopkeepers from Strathbane.

Charles Davenport was a nervous young man. "This is not what I expected, Angela," he said. "We're not in a very prominent position. And we're out of the range of the cameras."

"Oh, dear," said Angela. "The whole village is going to be watching to see me on television and there'll only be that horrible interview."

Hamish noticed Murdo at a central table with Anna Eskdale at his side. Then he saw Superintendent Daviot and his wife joining them.

Before the fiction awards, there were awards for various things to members of the sofa company's staff. The waiters were diligent at keeping glasses filled. Food was not to be served until the awards were over.

At last it was time for the fiction awards. The first award was for the children's writer at Angela's table. He was very drunk and weaved his way up to the podium where he

was violently sick. There was a delay while he was helped
off and taken somewhere in the nether regions. Angela had
stopped drinking wine a long time ago and Hamish was fed
up downing glasses of mineral water.

The next award was to "Scotland's foremost poet, Annie
McSporran, who, we are proud to say, works in our ac-
counts department."

A thin woman dressed head-to-foot in grey cashmere accepted a glass trophy in the shape of a sofa. She seized the
microphone. "I am very honoured," she said. "And I am going to read you some of my latest poems."

"Aw, naw!" cried a red-faced man. "Whar's the food!"

In a thin reedy voice, Annie began to declaim:

I was standing in ma kitchen,
A-combing of ma hair
When I saw a wee bit robin
And he gie me a stare.

Hamish forgot that he had hoped to do some detective
work. He was so sorry for Angela. The evening was turning
out to be a nightmare.

He turned to Charles. "Did you bring any of Angela's
books?"

"Yes, I've got a bag of them at my feet."

"Excuse me." Hamish slipped off and made his way to
where a man he identified as a producer from Strathbane
Television was standing. "How's it going?" he asked.

"Hellish," said the producer. "They're one of our main advertisers so we'll need to try to get something out of it."

"At my table is T. J. Leverage, who's written a grand detective story. She's from Lochdubh and I'm the local police sergeant, Hamish Macbeth. Let me introduce her. Give you a bit o' colour."

At the end of the awards to what turned out to be several undistinguished authors, the thin presenter stepped up to the microphone.

"We now have a special event," she said, "and then the banquet will be served."

"About time, too," yelled someone.

"Police Sergeant Hamish Macbeth! Step up to the podium."

"Make it short, laddie," said a man as Hamish made his way through the tables. "We're all starving."

Hamish seized the microphone. "We are honoured to have with us tonight T. J. Leverage, whose detective story *A Very Highland Murder* is set to top the charts. I am a police sergeant and can assure you that her grasp of police work is accurate. She has copies of her books and will sign them. Try to grab a first edition. Ladies and gentleman, a round of applause for T. J. Leverage."

Charles led Angela up to the podium. Hamish turned and saw a vase of flowers behind him. He lifted the flowers out and handed them to Angela.

"Well, Angela," said the presenter, elbowing Hamish aside with one bony elbow. "How are you enjoying the evening?"

"I am having a wonderful time," said Angela, "but as everyone is so hungry, that is all I have to say."

A great cheer followed her all the way back to the table, everyone delighted at the brevity of her speech. Water from the flowers Hamish had taken out of the vase dripped down her silk coat.

The Seven Steps had a well-deserved reputation for food, but as the sofa company was footing the bill, it turned out to be what Hamish damned as banquet food. The first course was a tiny vol-au-vent filled with mushrooms in a white sauce. This was followed by a piece of chicken breast flanked with two pieces of canned asparagus and ersatz mashed potato. The dessert consisted of one chocolate brownie and a dab of ice cream.

"Excuse me," said Hamish. He wanted to get through to the back premises to see if he could find anything fishy.

As he was about to leave the restaurant, a waiter barred his way, "May I help you, sir?"

"Gents," said Hamish curtly.

"On your left and down the corridor as you go out of the door."

Hamish walked along the corridor. He turned and looked back as he reached the toilet door. The waiter who had accosted him was watching him. Hamish went in and closed the door. He was pretty sure that when he came out again, that waiter would still be there, making sure he returned to the banquet.

He passed the urinals, went into the one stall, and closed

the door but did not lock it. He climbed up on the toilet seat and then clambered up on top of the cistern, praying it would take his weight.

Hamish stood awkwardly, his head and shoulders pressed against one wall and his feet braced against the other.

Then he realised it was going to be embarrassing if any guest entered the stall.

But after five minutes, he heard the door to the toilets open and a voice called, "Anyone here?"

The stall door opened. Hamish held his breath as he got a glimpse of the waiter. Then he listened until he heard the waiter go away. He slowly eased himself down, exited the gents, and went along the corridor to the back regions. He opened a few doors: storeroom full of crates of bottles and cans of vegetables in one, cleaning supplies in another. He came to a locked door at the end. It was only a Yale lock. He took out a thin strip of metal from the pocket of his evening suit, inserted it in the door, and sprang the lock. He let himself in and locked the door behind him just as he heard voices coming along the corridor. One voice said, "How could ye lose him?"

Hamish took out a pencil torch and flashed it around. He was in an office. There was a desk with a computer on it and a large safe in the corner. He stiffened as he heard them outside the door. They tried the handle and then walked away again.

Hamish sat down behind the desk and switched on the computer. It seemed to be full of innocent business files. He sighed. He was no expert. If there were any hidden files protected by a password, he wouldn't even know where to begin.

He opened the desk drawers. Nothing but stationery except for the bottom drawer, which was locked. Then he heard a woman's voice. "Are you sure you looked everywhere? What about here? Who has the key?"

Hamish looked around. There was a window behind the desk but it was barred. He went over and stood behind the door. It might just work. He was sure the female voice had belonged to Anna Eskdale. But he then thought that it was only in movies that no one looked round the door. He cautiously opened it, slid out into the corridor, dived into the nearest storeroom, and crouched down behind a pile of boxes.

He heard them come back, the jingle of keys, and then the office door being opened. "Nothing here," said a man's voice.

Anna's voice again. "Try the sheds at the back. That's the last place we want him to see."

Now, that's interesting, thought Hamish. He waited until he heard a door at the far end of the corridor open and close and then hurried back to the restaurant.

As he entered, it was suddenly like a game of musical chairs. It was as if all the waiters had suddenly frozen before going about their work.

"I've signed twenty books," said Angela, her face pink with pleasure.

"Good for you," said Hamish.

Anna Eskdale came into the restaurant. Before she sat down, her eyes flicked briefly to Hamish.

What was in those sheds at the back? wondered Hamish. He did not have any evidence to justify a raid on the premises.

Angela, crumpled up in a corner of the Mercedes on the road home, said, "I feel such a fool, Hamish."

"Why? Not your fault it was such a lousy evening."

"It's the money I wasted on this stupid outfit."

"You look grand."

"I could have worn an old sweater and jeans for all the difference it would have made."

"Now, then, you'll just have to get that man of yours to take you somewhere you can wear it again."

"I think the shop overcharged me."

"Why would they do that?" asked Hamish.

"Because the only time you read about authors' advances in the papers is when they get thousands. People think we're rolling in it."

"I'm sure they didn't. Relax, Angela. It's all over and you'll look grand on the telly."

"Can I watch it on Dick's big flat-screen?"

"Sure. I'll give you a spare key in case we're both out."

"Stopped leaving it up on the gutter?"

"Aye." Hamish had not but he planned to do so as soon as possible. His thoughts flew back to the restaurant. There had been an air of menace.

* * *

Dick was waiting up for Hamish. He handed him a brochure. "That's Beryl's rentals. I went round a few of them. Seems all aboveboard. How was the banquet?"

"Awful. But wait until you hear this."

Hamish told Dick about his adventures and ended by saying, "I'll phone Jimmy in the morning and see if he can think of some excuse to let us get a look at them. Sonsie and Lugs have a bit too much weight on them. I'm feeling restless. I think I'll take them for a walk."

"It's one on the morning!"

"I'm restless. The gale has died down and it's a grand evening."

The animals stretched and yawned and lazily followed him out onto the waterfront.

Hamish leaned against the waterfront wall and looked around. This was why, he reflected, he could never leave Lochdubh. The crescent of white cottages curved round to the humpbacked bridge at the end of the village. Smoke from peat fires rose lazily up into the vast starry sky. And it was that West Highland smell of home: tar and salt, evergreens and thyme, like no other smell in the world.

He suddenly found himself thinking of Elspeth Grant with an odd sort of longing. He could almost fancy he saw those strange silvery eyes of hers staring at him.

At the same time, Sonsie gave a low hiss. Hamish glanced down at his cat and then suddenly ducked. He heard a shot and the *wheesh* of a bullet passing overhead. He fell to the ground, then scrabbled for his mobile phone and called Strathbane, hugging his pets close to his body.

He felt a slow burn of anger. He was sure it was connected with that restaurant. Murdo Bentley was so cocky, he felt he could have a policeman killed without anything being traced back to him.

Jimmy arrived, heading a squad of policemen. He sent them off to search the village and the surrounding countryside. Settled in a chair in Hamish's kitchen, he opened his coat to reveal he was wearing his pyjamas underneath.

"Got hauled from my bed," said Jimmy. "Who do you think is trying to murder you?"

"Murdo Bentley," said Hamish, and told Jimmy about his adventures at the restaurant, ending with, "I wonder what's in those sheds at the back?"

"We've still not got enough for a search warrant," said Jimmy.

"And Daviot and his wife were guests of Murdo at the awards," said Hamish.

Dick, wrapped in a voluminous dressing gown, put a jug of coffee down on the table. "Nothing stronger?" asked Jimmy.

"You had the last o' the whisky last time you were here," said Dick.

"Could we say someone saw a man fleeing in the direction of the restaurant and search the damn place?" said Hamish.

"We might do that," said Jimmy slowly. "We could say we had an anonymous tip-off that a masked man was seen at the back of the restaurant. I'll round up the men."

There was a different manager from the one Hamish had met before who said he had a flat above the restaurant. He demanded a search warrant and was told it didn't apply when the life of a policeman had been threatened and that a masked man had been seen near the sheds at the back of the restaurant. The manager was ordered to open them up.

There were two long sheds at the back, both heavily padlocked. The manager seemed to take a long time finding the keys. At last the doors were opened.

But the sheds were empty. Under the glare of fluorescent light, there was not even a packing case to be seen.

"What are these used for?" demanded Jimmy.

"We keep stores in them from time to time," said the manager.

In one of the sheds, Hamish saw a door at the far end. "Where does that lead to?" he asked the manager.

The man shrugged. "Just out the back."

He selected a key, walked to the end of the shed, and opened the door. There was nothing outside but a stretch of moorland. Hamish sniffed the air. "There's a smell o' diesel," he said. "Any trucks been round the back here recently?"

The manager shook his head. His impassive features betrayed nothing other than a sort of weary interest.

Hamish unhitched a torch from his belt and went out and began to search the ground. The springy heather betrayed little. He was about to turn away when his torch shone on something. He bent down. It was a red silk ribbon. The manager's voice behind him made him jump. "Children sometimes play round here," he said.

"What is your name?" asked Hamish.

"Sergei Loncar."

The manager stretched out his hand for the ribbon. Hamish ignored him and popped it in a forensic bag.

"Come on," urged Jimmy. "There's nothing here, Hamish."

"And don't you find that odd?" asked Hamish.

"I'll get the men back to Lochdubh to see if your attacker left any clues." Jimmy stifled a yawn. "We'll talk more tomorrow."

Hamish was roughly awakened the next morning by Dick shaking him. "You're tae get ower tae Strathbane," he said. "Daviot's yelling for ye."

After he had hurriedly dressed, Hamish headed for Strathbane, leaving Dick to look after the dog and cat.

He hoped something had broken, that something incriminating had been found.

But when he saw the smile on secretary Helen's face, he knew there was trouble waiting for him in Daviot's office.

He entered. Blair was there, sitting on a chair at the side of the superintendent's desk, a smile on his fat face. Jimmy was standing in front of the desk. Hamish went to stand beside him.

"Good," said Daviot. "Now that we are all here, I want to make something very plain. The restaurant, the Seven Steps, has complained of police harassment. You, Macbeth, left the banquet to perform an illegal search of their premises. And…"

"And subsequently someone tried to kill me," said Hamish.

"Be quiet!" Daviot slammed both hands down on his desk. "This will stop now. Any member of my force who interferes again in the running of the restaurant will lose his job."

"Sir," said Jimmy, "thon maître d' has vanished and someone took his place on the plane. Hamish, here, heard them saying they hoped we wouldn't look in the sheds at the back. And…"

"And nothing. Nothing was found in the sheds. Probably Macbeth here was nearly hit by a stray bullet by a villager trying to kill a fox. Leave it alone. Now, off you go."

They all went out. "Better get back to your sheep," gloated Blair. "That's all you're good for, Macbeth."

"Pub. Ten minutes," whispered Jimmy, and Hamish nodded.

In the pub, to Jimmy's surprise, Hamish ordered a whisky. Hamish usually had strict rules about not drinking and driving.

"Something's awfy wrong here," said Hamish slowly.

"This is beyond Murdo being a member of the lodge and the Rotary and whateffer. Daviot's frightened."

"What?"

"I could smell the fear coming off him."

"I couldn't smell a thing," said Jimmy, lighting a cigarette.

"You can't smoke in here!" exclaimed Hamish.

"Barman turns a blind eye. So let's say our leader is frightened. Let's say that Murdo has got to him somehow. How on earth do we prove a thing like that?"

"You're in charge of the attempt to kill me. Whether Daviot likes it or not, there has to be a full report as to why all those officers were deployed searching the village and all around. Then you need to put in a report about the search of the sheds. So you type the lot up, I type my version up, you go to put it on his desk when he and Helen are out for lunch or something, and you bug his office."

"This isnae a James Bond movie. Where would I get a bug? Oh, we might have something in stores but I'd need tae sign in triplicate and anyway, I couldnae get one of those without the proper authorisation."

"It's all right. Dick's got the goods."

"Dick!"

"Aye, he won a James Bond quiz a while back and got all these gadgets."

"Are you sure about Daviot?"

"Can you think of any other reason why he should clamp down on the whole thing?"

"I'll give it a try," said Jimmy reluctantly. "But if he

finds this bug, it's all your fault. You haven't finished your whisky."

"I've gone off the idea. You have it."

Dick was out when Hamish returned to the police station, as were the dog and cat. Hamish searched his room until he found the spy equipment. He raced back to Strathbane after phoning Jimmy, who agreed to meet him on the road just outside of the town.

"This is the easiest one," said Hamish. "You put this bug anywhere on his phone line. You don't even need to take the phone apart. Then we park round the back of headquarters and listen in on this UHF transmitter."

"Is it legal?" asked Jimmy.

"Of course it isn't. These things are illegal unless you're outside the EU."

"Look, Hamish, the lunch hour is over. I'll need to wait until this evening. I haven't done my report anyway. Besides, tomorrow is my day off. So we can both listen then."

"All right," said Hamish reluctantly. "I'll meet you tomorrow morning."

Dick was back at the police station, rolling pastry and whistling as he worked.

"Did that other librarian get anything out of Hetty?" asked Hamish.

Dick blushed. "Not yet. She's working on it. I saw her at lunchtime."

Hamish explained why he had taken the spy equipment.

"What will you do if you find out Murdo's got something on him?" asked Dick.

"Confront him with it."

"He may have to resign. He's pretty useless anyway."

"Aye, but he's our useless," said Hamish. "A new broom might decide to sell this police station. Let's see how it goes. What are you making?"

"I thought some beef Wellington would be grand for dinner."

"I won't be around for dinner. I've got to go to Strathbane."

"It's not for you. I invited that librarian for dinner."

"Hetty?"

"No, the other one."

"Aha!"

"Aha, nothing," said Dick crossly. "You want information? This is ma way o' getting it. A lot o' people have called to see if you're all right. The trouble is there's that big dog fox that's been haunting the village. Folk think a bullet went astray and they're not going to own up. Oh, and Mr. Johnson phoned. He said there was a lassie at the hotel asking for ye."

Hamish phoned the hotel manager. "It's a tourist," said Mr. Johnson. "Wants to know all about the area. I gave her maps and brochures but she said maybe the local policeman might have a more personal knowledge. She's quite a looker."

"What's her name?"

"Katerina Drinsky."

Hamish's suspicions rose. A beautiful girl with a foreign name suddenly turns up and wants the local policeman.

"I'll be right up," he said.

He had expected a tall beauty like Anna Eskdale, but Katerina was small and a blonde with large blue eyes with a black ring round the iris. Mr. Johnson led him into the hotel lounge and introduced him.

"Why do you want a policeman to tell you about the neighbourhood?" said Hamish, removing his cap and sitting down opposite her.

"These leaflets are so...well...impersonal," she said.

Her voice had a lowland accent.

"Where are you from?" asked Hamish.

"My family is from Poland originally."

"You speak English very well."

She gave a gurgle of laughter. "I should. I am an English teacher. I was brought up in Scotland."

"And what is your interest in the Highlands at this cold, dreary time of year?"

"I have always been in love with the romance of the Highlands—Bonnie Prince Charlie, Robert Burns..."

"Robert Burns was an Ayrshire man."

"I meant Rob Roy."

"Rob Roy was a two-faced cattle thief and he hailed from the Trossachs, well south of here, in fact, about half an hour's drive from Glasgow."

She looked at him sadly. "I see I cannot deceive you."

"Why should you even try?" asked Hamish.

"The truth hurts."

"Try me."

"I have run away from my husband. This was as far as I could think to go. To be safe, I thought it might be a good idea to get friendly with a policeman."

"And where is your husband?"

"In Edinburgh. We are both second-generation Polish."

"So you could take out a restraining order against him."

"I did that. But he still frightens me."

Hamish took out his notebook. "Is Drinsky your married name?"

"Yes, but…"

"Address? The one in Edinburgh."

"One-Sixty-Five-B Herry Street," she said in a low voice.

"And whereabouts in Edinburgh is that?"

"Off Leith Walk."

"And are you really an English teacher?"

She burst into tears.

Hamish watched her carefully. He signalled to Mr. Johnson, who was lurking at the doorway.

"We need a box of tissues," he said.

A honey trap, thought Hamish. And a very clumsy one, too. When the box of tissues arrived, he said harshly, "Dry your eyes and stop acting!"

Then there came the sound of raised voices. A burly

young man erupted into the room and raced towards Katerina. "Slut!" he yelled.

Hamish tripped him up, dropped on top of him, and handcuffed him.

He looked up at Katerina. "Is this your husband?"

"Yes," she whispered.

So much for my bloody highland intuition, thought Hamish. He called Strathbane and said he was bringing someone in. A charge of attempted assault.

It turned out to be a weary day for Hamish. Katerina had inherited a Polish supermarket from her father. She had the money. Her husband was an unemployed layabout. She was trying to get a divorce and he had threatened to kill her. As he was considered a threat to her, he was locked up in the cells pending his appearance at the sheriff's court in the morning.

He had to type up his report, drive Katerina back to the hotel, and sit listening to her story of abuse, advising her to get a better lawyer than the one she had employed, before gently making his departure.

He phoned Jimmy and said he would meet him at nine o'clock. Wearing casual clothes, he set off for Strathbane, taking his pets with him.

Hamish met Jimmy in the car park at the back of police headquarters. "Have you put the bug in?" asked Hamish.

"Not yet. And his office door is locked."

"I'll do it. I'll say I've called to add a bit to that earlier report of attempted assault. Give me the bug."

"If you're caught," said Jimmy nervously, "then you have-nae seen me."

Hamish went straight into headquarters and made his way up the stairs to Daviot's office. He passed no one on the way.

He sprang the lock on the office door easily enough and let himself in.

The room was faintly lit by the glow from a streetlamp outside. He crawled under Daviot's desk and fitted the small bug to the telephone line.

He left quietly and softly made his way down the stairs. The door to the detectives' room was open and Blair was sitting at his desk. Hamish cursed under his breath. He darted past, hurtling down the stairs and out into the night. He hoped he and Jimmy would be able to find something out on the following day.

Meanwhile, Dick found his evening with Shona was getting off to a bad start, and he knew it was because he had over-done things. Her eyes had darted from the tall candles on the table, to the vase of red roses, to the crystal champagne glasses, and finally to the bottle of champagne in its ice bucket.

"You've gone to too much trouble," she said.

"I like to do things in style," said Dick. "Let me take your coat."

"Where's Mr. Macbeth?"

"Out somewhere."

"Will he be back soon?"

Dick suddenly realised that Shona thought she was looking at a scene set for seduction.

"Oh, Hamish will be here anytime now," he said, desperate to see her relax. "Don't be put off by all this. I'm used to giving Hamish the best. I'm a bit of a house husband."

To his relief, her face cleared. He served the starter of prawns Marie Rose along with slivers of toast. Then came the beef Wellington with little new potatoes and asparagus. Shona chattered on about people who had come to the library and the odd books they sometimes asked for.

Dick was just about to serve sherry trifle for dessert when he heard Hamish drive up. Couldn't the man have stayed away longer?

Hamish came in and blinked at the dinner arrangements. "Evening, Miss Macdonald," he said.

"Shona, please. What a marvellous cat!" Sonsie slouched in and disappeared into the living room followed by Lugs.

"I've kept back a bit of dinner for ye," said Dick sulkily.

"Don't worry," said Hamish. "I had fish-and-chips on the road home. But if that's sherry trifle, I'll have some of that." He pulled up a chair and sat down.

"So," said Hamish, "have you managed to winkle anything out of Hetty about Cyril?"

"Only that she seems to have forgotten that he dumped her," said Shona. "She's convinced that Cyril would have married her if he hadn't been killed."

Dick served the trifle.

"You're a lucky man, Hamish," said Shona, "having Dick spoil you like this."

Hamish looked at Dick and said, "Oh, we don't often dine like this." So that was it, he thought. Poor Dick. If he had told me he had fallen for the girl, I would have stayed away.

"I shouldn't have drunk so much," said Shona. "I've got to drive back to Braikie."

"I haven't had anything to drink," said Hamish. "I'll take you home, and Dick can drive your car over in the morning."

"That's so kind of you. Do you know Arthur Gibbs and Tony McVee?"

"I've heard of them," said Hamish. "Not villains, are they?"

"Oh, no, I went to a party at their house last year and everything was so beautiful."

After they had drunk coffee, Shona stifled a yawn. "I hate to end the evening," she said. "But I've eaten and drunk too much and I'm very sleepy."

"Right. I'll take you home," said Hamish.

Dick helped Shona into her coat. She smiled and said softly, "Thank you for a wonderful evening." She kissed him on the cheek. Hamish noticed the way Dick turned fiery red.

On the road to Braikie, Hamish said, "Dick's a good man. He'll make a wonderful husband."

"I know," said Shona. "He told me. You're a lucky man. I'm all for gay marriage."

"Whit! What's the silly numpty been saying?" roared Hamish.

"It's all right," said Shona. "I won't tell a soul. I suppose they can be cruel about that sort of thing in the police force."

"We are both heterosexual," said Hamish. "Why on earth did you think otherwise?"

"Dick said he was your house husband. I was a bit worried when I saw all the lengths he had gone to but he said he was used to giving you the best."

Hamish searched his mind for something to say to save Dick's face. At last he said, "It's all my fault. I'm so desperate to get information about Cyril that I told Dick to invite you and give you a slap-up dinner. He is a very conscientious police officer."

"He certainly went to a lot of trouble. I'm going to cook a meal for him and you as well."

"That's nice of you," said Hamish. "I'll tell him."

He dropped Shona at her home and returned to the police station, where Dick was dismally loading the dishwasher.

"You gave that poor lassie the idea we're a couple," said Hamish. "House husband, indeed. What did you expect her to think?"

"Not that anyway," said Dick. "What a disaster! She was nervous when she saw the champagne and everything and I realised she must be thinking I meant to seduce her."

"I began to wonder when she started talking about being at a party given by a couple o' gays. Don't you think she's a bit too young, Dick?"

"I know. I know. But every time I look at her, I forget."

Chapter Seven

A photograph is a secret about a secret. The more it tells you, the less you know.

—Diane Arbus

Jimmy and Hamish met up the next morning. They switched on the receiver and sat and waited. When Daviot's phone rang, they both jumped nervously. Helen's voice came loud and clear, "Superintendent Daviot's office."

"Put me through. It's Mrs. Daviot."

"You can hear both sides of the call," exclaimed Jimmy.

"Wheesht!" admonished Hamish.

Then a click as Daviot took the call. "What is it?" he demanded harshly.

In quavering tones, quite unlike her usual robust voice, Mrs. Daviot said, "I've invited the Baxters for dinner tomorrow night and I wondered…"

"Cancel it!"

"What? But I..."

"I said, cancel it."

The phone was slammed down.

Hamish and Jimmy stared at each other. Daviot had been under his domineering wife's thumb as long as they could remember.

The day dragged on as they listened to one official call after another. Daviot went out for lunch. "We should get a bite ourselves," said Jimmy.

"I don't want to risk missing anything," said Hamish.

"I'll nip round to the caff and get us a couple o' pies."

When Jimmy came back with the pies and two cardboard containers of coffee, Hamish said, "I feel dirty doing this. What if he finds that bug? They'll think terrorists and get the experts in and it'll all be traced back to Dick."

"Get it back tonight. May as well go on listening."

Daviot's phone rang, making them jump. Helen's genteel tones announced, "Mr. Bentley for you."

There was a long silence and then Daviot said wearily, "Put him through."

"And how are we today?" asked Murdo. "Being a good boy?"

"You'll ruin me," said Daviot bitterly. "There are questions being asked downstairs about why we dropped any investigation."

Murdo laughed. "They'll get over it. Just you go on doing as you're told or those photos of your wife go out on the Internet. Have a nice day."

Jimmy and Hamish stared at each other. Mrs. Daviot was a plump, grey-haired matron. What on earth had she been photographed doing?

"That's it," said Jimmy. "We go up there and say we've had an anonymous call that Murdo's holding incriminating photos of his wife."

"All he has to do is deny it," said Hamish. "Also, if he crumbles, he'll lose his job and God knows who we'll get instead. We've got to get these photos."

"How? They could be in his office in town or somewhere in that damn restaurant."

"There's a big safe in a room off the corridor at the back of the restaurant," said Hamish. "I'll try there first. The restaurant closes on Monday."

"There'll be burglar alarms all over the place. And you're no safe breaker."

"I'll think o' something," said Hamish desperately. "I don't remember the place being alarmed at the back. I'll get in there somehow and rummage through his desk. People sometimes leave a record of the safe code in their desks."

"And if you're caught?"

"I'll take Daviot down with me," said Hamish grimly.

"And just how will you do that?" sneered Jimmy. "All he has to say innocently is, *What photos?* You'll be out o' a job and Daviot'll still be in Murdo's clutches."

Hamish clutched his red hair. "I'll chust need to see what I can do," he shouted.

* * *

Dick received a call from Shona, inviting him and Hamish for dinner on Sunday evening. "I'd be delighted," said Dick. "I'll ask Hamish, but I don't know if he'll be free."

Shona said she looked forward to seeing him and rang off. She jumped as Hetty's voice came from behind her. "Were you using the library phone to make a personal call?"

Shona flushed. She hated the way Hetty always seemed to creep up on her. "It was just a quick call," she said defensively.

"Who to?"

Oh, for the courage to tell her to mind her own business. But Hetty was the chief librarian and had the power to sack, and jobs were scarce in Braikie.

"Just to that policeman, Dick Fraser. He entertained me to dinner and I have invited him and Mr. Macbeth to dinner at my place on Sunday evening."

"Then you'd better invite me as well," said Hetty. "He'll expect to see me and he'll be right disappointed if I'm not there."

Shona decided to serve as little alcohol as possible. Hetty was apt to get—well—*frisky* if she had too much to drink.

Hamish said he would go to Shona's with Dick, and Dick was relieved. He felt that the presence of Hamish would stop him from making a fool of himself.

And Hamish was glad to have something to distract him from worrying about the break-in he planned on Monday.

Before he left, Jimmy rang him to say that Katerina's

husband had been charged with assault, fined, and bound over to keep the peace. Hamish was somehow relieved that episode was over. It had reminded him that his famous intuition could be fallible.

Dressed in their best and carrying a good bottle of Merlot, Hamish and Dick arrived at Shona's home on the Sunday. It was as Dick remembered it, except this time the air was full of the smell of scorched food and Shona looked near to tears.

"It was to be duck à l'orange," she wailed. "I left it in the oven too long. Hetty's not here yet but she will sneer at me. Oh, how kind of you to bring wine, but it's not a good idea to let Hetty have too much."

"Lead me to the kitchen," said Dick. "I'm a dab hand at putting things together. There's a wee bit o' a gale blowing, so open the kitchen door and let the smell out. What have we here? Oh, look! You've a whole pack o' spaghetti." He opened the fridge. "And you've got a packet o' mince and tomatoes. Off you go, lassie, and leave it all to me. Wait a bit. I see you've got a carton o' tomato juice as well. I'll pour it into four glasses wi' a bit o' Worcestershire sauce and tell Hetty it's a Bloody Mary."

The doorbell rang. "That'll be Hetty," said Shona. "Dick, I don't know how to thank you."

"Just keep Hetty out of the kitchen."

Hamish was wondering if Shona had some sort of private income. Her apartment was the bottom half of a large Victorian villa. The living room contained a few good pieces of furniture. A coal fire burned on the hearth. A table was set for four at the bay window.

Shona ushered Hetty in, and Hamish rose to his feet. Hetty was wearing a long black velvet gown. Her heavy make-up was dead white and her thin mouth a slash of scarlet. She was wearing heavy false eyelashes.

"Why, it's the famous Hamish Macbeth," she said. She looked at him coyly. "Or should I say, the *infamous* Hamish Macbeth."

Dick bustled in with a tray of the Virgin Marys. "Bloody Marys all round," he said.

"Thanks, Dick," said Hamish. "This'll be my ration for the evening. I'm driving."

"I'll just see to the dinner," said Shona. "But cheers, everybody."

Hamish took a sip of his drink and realised immediately that there was no vodka in it.

Dick and Shona went off to the kitchen. "Sit down beside me," said Hetty, patting a place on the sofa next to her.

Hamish did as he was bid. "Have you got over your loss?" he asked.

"Oh, poor Cyril. We were to be married, you know."

"Were you going to move to Strathbane?" asked Hamish.

"We were going to travel the world," said Hetty. Then she let out a little scream. "There's a cockroach in my drink."

Hamish took it from her and peered at it. "It's one of your eyelashes," he said.

Hetty let out a squawk and took a little mirror out of her handbag. She turned away from Hamish and plucked off the remaining false eyelash. "Have my drink," said Hamish. "I've hardly touched it."

"Except with your lips," said Hetty with a leer.

"So," said Hamish, handing her his glass and putting her discarded glass on the floor at his feet, "how on earth were you going to afford to travel the world on a policeman's pay?"

"Cyril told me he was about to come into a lot of money."

"Where was it coming from?"

"I suppose some relative was due to die and leave him a lot of money. He was crazy about me, but men usually are."

"I thought *he* dumped *you*," said Hamish.

"Not really," said Hetty. "Let's talk about something else. You're not married, are you?"

"Not yet."

Hetty edged closer to him on the sofa. "There's always hope," she said. "Every cloud has a silver lining."

"How true," said Hamish. "And it never rains but it pours. It's an ill wind that…"

"Are you taking the piss?" demanded Hetty.

"Wouldn't dream of it."

"Take your places at the table," came Shona's voice. "First course coming up."

Dick carried in a tray with plates of smoked salmon. Shona followed him carrying a bottle of white wine wrapped in a cloth. She looked windswept, having fled out the back and round to the supermarket to buy bottles of non-alcoholic wine.

Hetty began to look sulky. Where was the buzz from alcohol that she had been looking forward to?

She stood up abruptly. "I've left my cigarettes in the car. Back in a minute."

Hetty went out to her car. She had bought a bottle of vodka earlier that day. She sat in the driver's seat, wrenched open the top, and took a long satisfying swig. She downed another one and began to feel irresistible. As she eased her way out of the car, she began to think of Hamish as a marital prospect.

"Get your cigarettes?" asked Hamish when Hetty rejoined them.

"Silly me," said Hetty, sitting down and patting him on the knee. "They were in my handbag all along."

Why is it that people think vodka doesn't smell? thought Hamish.

"Tell me about yourself," said Hetty, her prominent eyes fastened on Hamish's face.

"You've hardly touched your salmon," said Hamish.

"I don't really like smoked salmon," said Hetty. "I'll save my appetite for the next course." She downed her glass of wine in one great gulp.

"I'll get the next course," said Shona. Dick rose to his feet as well.

Hetty waggled a finger at Dick. "Naughty, naughty! You look so grim I do believe you're jealous."

Her narcissism was amazing, reflected Hamish. She probably had not even noticed that Shona was a very pretty girl.

"This is not my idea of cooking," said Dick, twisting the lid off a jar of Bolognese sauce that he had told Shona to get in the supermarket. "But it would ha' taken too long to do the real thing. I'll just add the tomatoes and chopped mushrooms and garlic to make it seem a bit mair homemade."

He deftly drained the spaghetti onto four deep dishes, put a generous helping of the sauce on each plate, and loaded them onto a serving trolley with a bottle of red non-alcoholic wine and a bowl of grated Parmesan cheese.

As they entered the room, Hamish leapt to his feet, shouting, "A rat! There's a rat crawling up my leg!"

Hamish was well aware that the "rat" was in fact Hetty's stockinged foot.

Hetty had withdrawn her foot and now looked sulkily under the table. "It's your imagination," she said. "There's nothing there."

Hamish sat down. "Well, if I feel the beastie again, I'll stamp on it and break its back."

Hetty stared in suppressed fury at the plate of spaghetti Bolognese in front of her. She did not hate the taste. She hated the fact that she had never mastered the dexterity of eating it properly. Besides, the brief euphoria engendered by those two swigs of vodka had ebbed away.

She rose from the table. "Excuse me," she said.

"You know where the bathroom is, Hetty," said Shona.

"I need something from my car."

"It's a cold night," said Hamish maliciously, because he knew exactly what it was that Hetty wanted. "Tell me what it is, give me your keys, and I'll get it for you."

"No!" shouted Hetty and slammed out of the room. Once at her car, she seized the vodka bottle, then hurried back into the house and through to the bathroom at the back. She sat down on the lid of the pan, opened the bottle, and proceeded to drink.

Soon Hetty could feel the alcohol surging through her veins like elixir. She finished the vodka, opened the bathroom window, and hurled the empty bottle into the garden. She was passing the kitchen on her way back when she saw a bottle of brandy lying next to the coffee cups on the kitchen table. The temptation was too much. She poured herself a large tumbler of brandy and downed it.

Shona was just saying nervously, "She's been away an awfully long time. I'd better go and look for her," when Hetty appeared in the doorway, looked blindly around, and then collapsed unconscious on the floor.

"We'd better get her to the hospital and get her pumped out. She's done it this time," said Hamish. "Phone for an ambulance, Dick. I don't want to take her myself. In the meantime, we'd better walk her up and down."

Fortunately the ambulance arrived after only five minutes—fortunate because Hetty showed no signs of regaining consciousness.

They followed the ambulance in the Land Rover to Braikie hospital. They didn't return to Shona's flat until Hetty's stomach was pumped out and they were told she would be all right.

It had transpired to Hamish's relief that this was not the first time that Hetty had been taken to hospital in similar circumstances, because he was sure Hetty would try to put the blame on Shona.

Shona looked so worried and distressed that Dick cursed Hetty with all his heart.

"If you ever feel like inviting us to dinner again," he said, "make sure she doesn't know about it."

Monday evening arrived and with it a nervous Angela Brodie escorted by her husband to watch her TV appearance.

Dick settled them in the living room with drinks and snacks. "Here comes your big moment, Angela," he said, switching on the television.

After a long noisy advertisement for sofas on sale— "are sofas never *not* on sale," muttered Hamish—film of guests arriving at the banquet appeared. No Angela. Then green room interviews with the winners, but the interview with Angela appeared to have been cut. More sofa advertisements, followed by a long introductory speech by the head of the sofa company. The camera panned occasionally round the guests but Angela was always out of range. She leaned forward in her chair. Surely, they would feature

Hamish's impromptu presentation. But nothing. Absolutely nothing.

"Bastards!" said Dick.

"Never mind, Angela," said Hamish. "You're a real writer, unlike the award winners."

"It'll teach me never to waste money again," said Angela. "I feel like an absolute fool."

"Come on home, dear," said Dr. Brodie. He gave her a hug.

After they had left, Hamish began to sort out his burglary tools. "Are you sure you want to go through with this?" asked Dick nervously. He was worried that if Hamish was caught, Strathbane would have a good reason to shut down the police station. "I'll come with you," he said suddenly. "You'll need someone to stand guard."

"I don't want you to risk getting caught as well," said Hamish. "Who'd look after Sonsie and Lugs if we both end up in prison?"

"If there's any risk o' that, I'll clear off and leave you to it."

"All right. Just make sure you do."

They set out at two in the morning. Hamish was glad that there was a thick covering of cloud over the moon. They drove in Dick's little car and parked it up a grassy track some way away from the restaurant. Both were wearing black clothes.

They made their way silently to the restaurant over the fields at the back. "Keep away from any CCTV cameras," whispered Hamish. "At the first sign of trouble, get yourself as far away as possible."

Dick crouched down behind a clump of bushes near the sheds. "If I hear or see someone coming, I'll give an owl hoot," he said.

Hamish went off at a run. When he reached the back door of the restaurant, he flicked on a pencil torch and scanned the outside of the building. He cursed when he saw a yellow burglar alarm box high up on the wall. He climbed up a drainpipe and cut the wires, praying that the device was as old as it looked and not liable to go off the moment it was tampered with.

He climbed down again and then spent twenty minutes picking the door lock. He moved silently into the corridor, shutting the door behind him. He found the door to that office and worked on the lock there until the door sprang open.

Hamish went immediately to the desk. He searched the drawers in the hope that the code to the safe was somewhere. There was a thick black appointments book in the centre drawer. He opened it and searched through it, his torch flickering over the pages. He was about to put it back when he saw several of what appeared to be phone numbers on the inside back page. Hamish remembered that people often disguised their PINs or safe numbers by putting an area code in the front.

There was one that interested him. It read 0151-78006923.

He quickly memorised the number without the area code, then stood up and turned to the safe. He put in the code and could hardly believe his luck when the steel door opened.

Resisting the temptation to search the ledgers, he concentrated on looking for photographs. He was about to give up but then wondered if they might be in one of the ledgers. He took them out, one by one, and began his search. In the fourth ledger, he found a packet of photographs and computer disks. He flicked his torch over them. He established that they were the compromising photographs of Mrs. Daviot. He hurriedly put the photos in his pocket, returned the ledgers, and was about to make his escape when he decided he had better search the computer in case they were stored there as well.

The computer, a laptop, was password-protected. There was a large old railway clock on the wall behind Hamish, sonorously ticking the precious seconds away while he looked feverishly in the book again to see if a password had been noted.

His eye fell on ViOdeR8, scrawled in tiny print in the very corner. He typed it in and the computer opened up. He would have loved to take time to search through it, but all he wanted were the photographs. He found them and winced at the images of Mrs. Daviot in the arms of Paolo Gonzales. Hamish quickly deleted them. He then went to

Google and put in a request—how to disable a computer? He followed the instructions with a feeling of malicious satisfaction. His task completed, he was just switching off the machine when he heard the sound of a vehicle arriving at the front of the restaurant. He double-checked the photos and disks in his pocket, pulled a black balaclava over his face, and ran out of the back door just as a Land Rover with a light on the roof came round the building.

Hamish fled. He was a champion hill runner but he knew where he would have to go to shake them off. He headed straight for Crimmond's Bog, a marshy area near the back of the restaurant. As he gained the edge of the bog, a bullet whistled past his ear. He prayed he could remember the one safe track through the bog.

He heard yells behind him and glanced round. The Land Rover had hit the bog and was sinking fast. Hamish gained the other side of the bog, running as fast as a deer, circling round until he reached the main road. He hoped Dick had had the sense to get clear. But just as he reached the road, the moon shone down and Dick's little car came slowly along.

Hamish flagged him down and hurtled into the passenger seat. "Fast as you can," he said. He lay back in the seat, his heart thudding like a piston.

Back at the station, Dick looked at the photographs and blushed to the roots of his hair. "Who'd ha' thought it?" he exclaimed. "I wonder where Gonzales is now?"

"He's probably in that convenient bog," said Hamish. "Even if whoever was chasing me knew about it, they would have forgotten in their desperation to get me."

"I found this," said Dick, holding out a crumpled bit of paper. "It was caught in the bushes. It's an address."

Hamish smoothed it out and read "Olga Sobinski, 4, Murray Way, Strathbane."

"We'll call there and see what goes on," he said. "But we'd better get Jimmy over here and discuss how we're going to confront Daviot. Let's look at the CDs and make sure Mrs. Daviot's the only one on them." This turned out to be the case.

"A woman wi' a big arse like that shouldnae wear a thong," said Dick dolefully.

Chapter Eight

☠

Love is like the measles; we all have to go through
with it.

— Jerome K. Jerome

Jimmy arrived in response to Hamish's urgent summons the
following morning.

"Any report of a break-in at the restaurant last night?"
asked Hamish.

"Not that I've heard. Was that you?"

"Aye and they damn near tried to kill me," said Hamish.
"I've got the photos."

"Give me a strong coffee and let me see them."

As Dick prepared the coffee, Hamish put the photographs down on the kitchen table.

"Oh, michty me," wailed Jimmy. "What do we do now?
We don't want the man to lose his job."

"We'll need to let him know that he doesn't have anything more to fear from Murdo. Then we get a search warrant and take that damn restaurant apart. Now, Dick found a crumpled piece of paper with an address in Strathbane. I'd like to call there first."

"Why?"

"When we were searching in the sheds, I found a piece of red ribbon."

"So what?"

"Just a hunch that they might be trafficking women as well as drugs."

"Do you need me?" asked Dick plaintively.

"Yes, I need you and the dog and cat," said Hamish. "The bastard might come over here. They'll suspect it was me. Let's go."

They parked outside a tall villa on Murray Way. "If it's part o' Murdo's organisation," said Hamish, "they might recognise me. You go, Jimmy. Ask for Olga and take it from there."

Jimmy groaned. "I could do wi' a dram to take the edge off."

"You don't need the edge off," said Hamish. "Get on with you!"

"I sometimes think you don't realise you're speaking to your superior officer," grumbled Jimmy.

"Oh, hurry up, *sir*," said Hamish.

Jimmy went up and rang the bell. The door opened and a tall Slavic-looking woman smiled at him. "Come in," she said.

Thanking his stars that no one ever took him for a member of the police force, Jimmy went into a reception area where several girls in various stages of undress were sitting about.

"So, what is your pleasure, sir?"

Jimmy contrived to look like a businessman who had suddenly got cold feet. "Can I come back later?" he said, and fled out the door.

He got in the car. "It's a brothel. It's Blair's day off. I'll get it raided right now."

"And get a watch on Murdo's house and restaurant," said Hamish. "Put up roadblocks and get a watch on the airports, and trains."

"Don't give me orders," snapped Jimmy.

They waited anxiously until the police arrived in force. "Right, here we go," said Hamish.

The raid was successful. Twelve Eastern European women were hustled out into police vans along with the tall woman who turned out to be Olga.

The premises were being searched when Police Inspector Harold Simms hurried up to Jimmy. "Mr. Daviot on the phone," he said. "You're to call off the search."

"Carry on," said Jimmy grimly. "I'm going to see him."

Leaving Dick behind, Jimmy and Hamish drove to police headquarters and went straight up to Daviot's office. Ignoring Helen's squawk of, "You can't go in there!" they thrust her aside and walked into Daviot's office. The superintendent's face was paper white.

"I've told Simms to call off the search," he shouted, leaping to his feet.

Hamish took out the packet of photographs, opened it, and spread the photos on the desk.

Daviot glanced at them and buried his head in his hands. "Helen may be listening," said Hamish in a low voice. "Send her away."

"What shall I say?" asked Daviot.

Hamish went and opened the door. "Helen, Mr. Daviot says you're to go to the florist's immediately and send a dozen red roses to his wife."

He stood there until Helen put on her coat, picked up her handbag, and left.

"Now we can talk," said Hamish, going back into the superintendent's office. "You have nothing to fear from Murdo Bentley now, sir. We've put out an all-points alert to pick him up. His restaurant and office are being raided."

"I must resign," said Daviot wretchedly.

"Now, there's no reason for that," said Jimmy soothingly. "Nobody knows about thae photos."

"What if that man Gonzales appears?" asked Daviot.

"As to that," said Hamish, "in the next few days we'll get that bog near the restaurant drained. But take it from me, that creature is dead."

"How could my wife behave like a slut?" asked Daviot.

"Easy," said Hamish. "They probably slipped her a drug."

"She keeps saying she can't remember anything about it."

"Mrs. Daviot's probably telling the truth," said Jimmy. "They probably slipped her a date-rape drug, dressed her up like a tart, and got Gonzales to do his bit. My guess is that Gonzales tried to blackmail Murdo."

Daviot's phone rang. "I'll get that," said Jimmy. He listened and then his face darkened. "Keep a watch on all the airports and roads," he ordered.

He put the phone down and turned to Daviot. "They can't find Murdo. They got a haul o' drugs from his restaurant, and one of the girls from the brothel who speaks English said they were all from the Ukraine. They were promised jobs in the restaurant and when they arrived, their passports were taken away and they were forced into prostitution. I've got to go, sir, and join the search. Burn those photos, be nice to the missus, and neither Hamish nor I will say a word."

"I don't know how I can ever thank you," said Daviot. "How did you get these photos back?"

"Best not to ask," said Hamish. "We'd better go and join in the hunt."

All that long day, the search went on. All Murdo's staff, with the exception of Anna Eskdale, who had disappeared along with Murdo, had been rounded up.

A weary Hamish returned late to his police station and told Dick about the developments.

"I've got some nice venison stew for you," said Dick. "I wonder where the bastard has got to?"

"And I wonder who tipped him off," said Hamish grimly. "Jimmy found out that when they got to his office, the safe was lying open, and so was a back door to the place. He can't use his credit cards but it's my bet he had money in that safe."

He sat down at the kitchen table. Dick put a plate of stew in front of him. Hamish raised a forkful to his mouth and then froze. "The docks!" he exclaimed. "I wonder if Jimmy thought of the docks. There are a lot of villains down there. Murdo could have paid someone to take him off by boat."

Hamish dashed off to the office. Dick put his dinner in the microwave, ready to reheat the food.

He finally came back and slumped down at the table. "Jimmy remembered the docks but maybe too late. Murdo kept a converted fishing boat down there and it's gone. The coastguard has been alerted."

Dick heated Hamish's dinner and put it back on the table. "I wonder how far he got," said Hamish.

Murdo was heading across the Minch, the strait that divides the mainland from the outer isles. His plan was to hide out on one of the remote islands until he guessed the search would not be so intense. Anna Eskdale stood behind him in the wheelhouse, staring gloomily out at the heaving black waves. They were in the middle of the Minch when the engine suddenly coughed and died. Murdo cursed. He normally never skippered the boat himself, and he had assumed that the villain he usually employed had put enough petrol in it.

"We can't bucket about here waiting for the coastguard to pick us up," said Anna. "We'd better take to the dinghy."

They lowered the dinghy into the water. Anna took over and started the outboard and they went off, crashing through the waves.

It was a perfect morning on the island of Eriskay when widow Martha Hibbert went out to feed her chickens. She was a tall, bony woman who gained a very small income writing steamy romances. Martha had moved from London after the death of her husband ten years ago to enjoy the solitude of the Outer Hebrides. She was just about to turn away to go back into her low white croft house when she saw a man and a woman approaching across the heather in the pale grey light of dawn. The sun did not rise until around ten in the morning. So far north in the British Isles means little daylight in the autumn and winter months. The man was carrying a small travel bag.

Murdo and Anna were both soaked to the skin. Murdo's plan was to take over some household at gunpoint until they dried out and worked out what to do.

But Martha approached them with a welcoming smile. "Did you fall in the water?" she asked. "Come in and dry yourselves and I'll make some tea."

Murdo decided to leave his gun in his pocket.

"That's kind of you," he said. "We had a bit of an accident on the boat."

Martha ushered them into the parlour and built up the

fire. "I'll just get you some dry clothes," she said. "Your wife can have some of mine and I've still got some of my late husband's clothes."

Martha, before she went to look out clothes for them, went into the kitchen where she had a small television set. She had recognised the pair. She put the television in the bottom of a cupboard.

When she returned with the clothes and towels, they were huddled over the fire. "I'll leave you to get dressed," she said. "Then I'll hang your clothes out to dry. It's going to be a grand day."

"Have you a television set here?" asked Anna.

"No, I don't watch the telly and I don't read newspapers. I came up here to get away from the world."

Anna and Murdo stripped and changed, Anna into a shirt and a pair of corduroy trousers and Murdo into a sweater and overalls.

"Harmless biddy," said Murdo. "Let's go along with it for a bit."

Martha returned and gathered up their wet clothes. "Come through to the kitchen," she said, "and I'll make you some breakfast. But first, have a cup of tea."

Murdo and Anna were both exhausted. They gratefully accepted their mugs of strong tea.

Suddenly they felt themselves losing consciousness. Murdo tried to struggle up but then fell across the table while Anna slumped to the floor.

Martha quickly opened the travel bag. She spread the

contents out on the kitchen counter. There were wads of fifty-pound banknotes and various passports in various names. She then searched Murdo until she found the gun. After that, she searched Anna and found another gun. Martha returned everything along with one gun back into the bag and locked it all up in a small safe in her bedroom. She studied Murdo's gun. It was a Smith & Wesson. Her late sister had lived in Texas, and when Martha had visited, her sister had taken her to a gun range and shown her how to load and use a Smith & Wesson.

She picked up the telephone to contact the police and then replaced the receiver.

Times had been hard for Martha recently, and her publisher had just refused to renew her contract. That money would come in handy. It had been a long time since she could afford a trip to the mainland to buy new clothes.

She had hoped the solitude of the island would inspire her but somehow the writing seemed harder than ever. The simple life, she had discovered, was all right for townies with money, playing at being sort of Marie Antoinettes.

The weather was quiet that day, but usually Martha lived in a cacophony of noise from waves and wind. She had begun to talk to herself, even when she went to the shop, and the locals had begun to avoid her.

That money could also maybe get her as far as London to see her useless agent. Martha began to giggle. She could even take the gun with her and see his frightened face.

But what to do with this precious pair in the meantime?

She went out to the shed and came back with a wheelbarrow and a length of rope and duct tape. First she tied up Murdo and taped his mouth before sliding him onto the wheelbarrow and taking him out to the shed, where she tipped him onto the floor. She returned and completed the same process with Anna. Then she securely padlocked the shed.

Martha wondered whether to call on the island's doctor for a new supply of sleeping pills, having used up what she had drugging the pair. Then she realised happily that she could now afford whisky, and whisky was better than sleeping pills any day.

But how had they arrived? She walked down to the beach and saw the dinghy. She went back and got a hammer and smashed holes in the bottom, then waded into the water, pushed it out to sea, and waited until it sank.

Singing to herself, she returned to her croft house. But what about her six hens? She could get a neighbour to look after them, but what if that precious pair woke up and started banging about the shed?

Sadly, she caught each hen and wrung its neck and put the dead birds in the freezer.

Dressed carefully in her best clothes, and carrying Murdo's travel bag, Martha got into her old Ford and drove across the causeway to Barra to wait for the ferry to the mainland.

A couple of weeks later, Jimmy, Hamish, Dick, and Blair along with a forensic team and several police officers gathered at the harbour in Lochdubh as Archie Maclean's fishing boat appeared, towing Murdo's boat behind him.

They waited impatiently while the forensic team boarded Murdo's boat. "She wass chust bobbing about on the Minch," said Archie. "But the dinghy's missing."

It soon transpired that the boat had run out of petrol. "They could be anywhere," grumbled Blair. "I'll phone the coastguard."

Hamish took Archie aside. "If you landed in the middle o' the Minch in a dinghy, where would you head?"

"Well…" Archie pushed back his cap and scratched his grey hair. "She was in the Little Minch so maybe Barra."

"Or," said Hamish, "they might want to land where there aren't many folk."

"There's Eriskay. Only about one hundred and fifty folk there," said Archie.

"Whit are you daein' wi' all them polis?" screeched a voice from Archie's small cottage.

"The wife," said Archie. "Better go."

Hamish went in to the police station and got down a pile of maps to study. Dick, who had followed him in, said, "Any guesses?"

"I'd like a look at Eriskay."

"D'ye think Blair will let you go?"

"No. He won't want me around anywhere. You stay here and cover for me."

"Bring me back a bottle o' that famous whisky."

"What famous whisky?"

"You've forgotten. That's where the SS *Politician* struck the rocks wi' a cargo o' thousands of bottles of whisky. That's why Compton Mackenzie wrote *Whisky Galore* and they made that film."

Hamish drove to Oban and caught the ferry to Barra. From Barra, he drove to Eriskay. He turned over in his mind what he knew of Eriskay. It had once been under Norse occupation for four hundred years—hence the name, the Norse for "Eric's Island." On the twenty-third of July, 1745, the French ship *Du Teillay* put ashore Bonnie Prince Charlie. He met Alexander of Boisdale, who urged him to go home. Charles is reported to have said, "I am come home, sir," and then sailed to the mainland and raised his standard at Glenfinnan. If only he had gone home again, reflected Hamish. So many lives would have been saved.

He went into the village of Ain Baile and asked if anyone had seen any strangers, but no one had. He remembered how faulty his intuition had been about the woman from Edinburgh. Murdo and Anna could be anywhere.

Hamish decided that maybe they would have picked an isolated house. He drove slowly round, stopping occasionally to get out and search the beaches for any sign of a dinghy. The light was fading fast and the wind was beginning to howl.

He decided to try the west of the island and then give up. He parked the Land Rover beside a curve of white sand and got down and shone his torch. The gale was now screaming, and it was bitterly cold. Great black breakers from the Atlantic pounded the shore. He was about to turn away when his torch lit a piece of wreckage. He hurried down and examined it. It had definitely come off some sort of boat. He turned his back on the heaving sea. There was a croft house a little bit away from the beach. It was dark and silent, and no smoke rose from the chimney.

Hamish went up and knocked at the door. There was no reply. He went round to the kitchen and shone his torch in the window. One kitchen chair had fallen over. He picked the lock and let himself in, calling, "Police! Anybody here?"

But he knew somehow from the silence that the house was deserted.

He switched on the light in the kitchen. There was a single muddy tyre track leading to the kitchen door. He went into the living room and switched on the light there. A bookcase contained a series of romances by Martha Hibbert. There was a computer and printer on the table along with a pile of typed manuscript pages. He then went along to a small bedroom. The wardrobe door was open, as were some of the drawers on a chest of drawers, as if someone had packed hurriedly.

He went back to the kitchen and opened the door. Outside, there was a damp area of mud and the single tyre track running through it.

He pointed his torch towards the shed. The door was fastened with a strong padlock. He went back to the Land

Rover, fetched a pair of bolt cutters, then went back to the shed and severed the padlock.

Hamish shone the torch on the two bound bodies on the floor—Murdo and Anna.

He felt Murdo's neck for a pulse and found none. He guessed he had probably died of a combination of cold and dehydration. He then bent over Anna. There was a pulse but it was faint. He hurriedly unbound her and ripped the tape from her mouth. He heaved her up, carried her into the house, and laid her down on the bed in the bedroom, noticing there was an electric blanket, which he switched on.

Hamish went into the living room and desperately phoned for help. He realised that no helicopter could land in the howling gale. He saw a list of numbers above the phone on the wall. One of the numbers was for a Dr. Trapesy in the village. He phoned and asked the doctor to come immediately.

Returning to Anna with a glass of water, he dribbled a little of it into her mouth. Her eyes fluttered open.

"Why did you kill Cyril?" asked Hamish.

"Who?"

"Cyril Sessions. The policeman."

"Not us," she said faintly. "Murdo?"

"Just rest. The doctor's on his way."

Her eyes closed again.

Hamish paced up and down until he heard a car arrive. The doctor, a small plump man with a shock of white hair, bustled in. Hamish showed him through to the bedroom.

He felt for a pulse. "She's gone. I'll try to get her back." He took a defibrillator out of his capacious case and got to work. At last, he shook his head. "She's a gonner."

"There's another body in the shed," said Hamish. "Does Martha Hibbert own this place?"

"Aye, the writer. A bittie scary. Soft in the head."

"The dead couple are Murdo Bentley and Anna Eskdale," said Hamish. "We've been hunting for them."

Martha had checked into a modest bed-and-breakfast in Fulham in London. She found her agent was on holiday and not due back for a week. She had meant to visit her editor first, but she was always mysteriously unavailable. Martha was determined to wait. It was surely the useless agent's fault that her books were no longer to be published.

At last, his assistant said he had returned. Martha walked to the basement her agent, Harold French, used as an office.

Harold French looked dismayed when he learned Martha was coming to see him. He not only detested Martha, he detested writers, who all seemed to think they were Dickens. Harold had been a schoolteacher in a comprehensive when his father died and bequeathed him the agency. At first Harold was delighted to get away from horrible children and what he sourly considered Trotskyist teachers. The jewel in the crown of his clients—of which he had few left—was a deceased bestselling detective writer who had bequeathed him the rights to her books. His father had left him not only the office but also a large villa on the Thames along with a portfolio of stocks and shares. This engendered a comfortable enough income to let him indulge in being rude to authors. He was a tall rangy man with black hair and an aquiline nose. He had been married and divorced three times, all on the grounds of his cruelty. He had fired his assistant after she had told him of Martha's impending arrival for no other reason than to see if he could make her cry.

He beamed at Martha and prepared to enjoy himself by putting the boot in.

"Sit down, my dear," he said. "Have you come all the way from the Hebrides?"

"Yes, we really must talk. I have been told that they are not going to publish any of my books. Why is that?"

"Well, you've gone out of fashion. In fact, you have been damned as old-fashioned. Lots of heaving bosoms but no explicit sex. Lots of steam but nothing under the kettle, so to speak. Maybe not enough experience?" He gave a self-satisfied chuckle as the colour mounted to Martha's cheeks.

"What if I write a detective story?" said Martha. "They seem to be very popular."

"Do you read many?"

"I watch *Midsomer Murders.*"

"That pap. Oh, forget it. I'm afraid I have to tell you that your writing days are over."

"But I have an idea for a detective story in my handbag."

"Really, Martha, I would like to talk to you longer but…"

His voice faded away as Martha took a gun out of her handbag. "Now, let's not be silly," he said, reaching for the phone.

Martha shot him in the chest and then walked over and shot him in the head.

She had brought a travel bag with her. She opened it, took out new clothes from Marks & Spencer, and began to put them on and then put the bloodstained clothes in the bag.

Martha felt a feeling of exultation. She considered every one of her romances a work of art. Now for her editor. After she had dumped the travel bag.

She blamed the new editor that had been assigned to her by her publishers, Ferris & Ferris. Although Martha had never met her, she had seen photographs of the woman on her website and had not liked what she had seen. Called Freddy Mulkin, she was plump with a great round face and black hair streaked with pink highlights.

Freddy Mulkin was a compulsive overeater. As soon as lunchtime came around, she headed for the nearest McDonald's, ordered two Big Macs, two fries, and a milk shake. She carried them over to a table by the window, just vacated by a couple, already salivating over the lunchtime treat in store.

She was biting into a Big Mac when a woman sat down opposite her and said, "Mizz Mulkin?"

"What? Who are you?" demanded Freddy, feeling like a lioness balked of her prey.

"I am Martha Hibbert."

"Am I supposed to know you?"

"You are my editor, you useless piece of garbage. You had the temerity to tell me that my books were no longer going to be published."

"Oh, that Martha Hibbert. Don't glare at me." The decision not to publish Martha's books had come down from the senior editor, but Freddy, like the recently deceased literary agent, liked power over authors. "Look, your sales figures are abysmal. We can't go round carrying deadwood."

A man, operating a road drill, started to dig up the pavement outside.

Martha smiled as Freddy gave a massive shrug of her shoulders and greedily took a huge bite out of her Big Mac.

She opened her handbag, took out the gun under the cover of the table, and shot Freddy right in her large stomach.

Freddy let out a long wail of pain and terror, but the noise was drowned by the cacophony of the road drill.

Martha left and went to the British Museum, where she sat on the steps and felt all the power and exultation seeping out of her body.

She knew that sooner or later, the police would scan all the CCTV cameras in the area. As she had not read any newspapers, she did not know they were already looking for her.

Martha got sadly to her feet and hailed a cab. "Scotland Yard," she said.

* * *

Elspeth Grant was called into the news editor's office. "I know you won't want to do it," he said, "but it's a great story. Drugs and human trafficking up in the Highlands and now some woman up in Eriskay killed two of the leaders, went down to London, shot her agent and her editor, and then turned herself in at Scotland Yard."

"What am I supposed to add to it?" asked Elspeth. "There's been yards of it on television already."

"But you always get something no one else has. Get over to Eriskay and do a colour piece about what the locals think of her."

Hamish and Dick with the dog and cat sat up on the hills above Lochdubh, having a picnic, to get away from the press. Jimmy had just phoned Hamish on his mobile to tell him about Martha Hibbert.

"She must ha' been stark staring mad," said Dick, munching on a ham sandwich.

"It can happen to people from the cities," said Hamish. "They take off for some remote spot, and sooner or later the loneliness eats into them. The locals can be standoffish, although I don't know what they're like on Eriskay. They either end up drinking too much, or they get depressed and start talking to themselves. Usually a lot of them are too proud to admit even to themselves that they couldn't hack it."

"Martha's getting a lot of sympathy from other disappointed authors," said Dick. "And evidently her books are selling like mad."

"Well, they say, the worse the writer, the bigger the ego," said Hamish. "Not everyone's been rounded up. The Campbell brothers, for instance. And I worry about thon woman Beryl Shuttleworth. Nothing has been linked to her and yet she employed two men who probably got rid of Gonzales."

"They're still going through masses of paperwork," said Dick. "Maybe they'll find a connection."

"I might call on her and invite her out to dinner," said Hamish.

"Be careful," urged Dick. "She might shoot you under the table like Martha did to that poor editor."

"I'll try anyway," said Hamish. "We'd better pack up. It's getting dark already and I can smell rain coming."

"What about consulting the seer, Angus Macdonald?" asked Dick. "He picks up a lot o' gossip."

"You go," said Hamish. "There's another thing. Just before she died, Anna said they didn't kill Cyril."

"So what. Maybe they didn't but as sure as hell they got him killed."

"It still niggles at me."

Dick set off for the seer's cottage later that day. Angus Macdonald always expected some sort of gift, and Dick had a cupboard full of chocolates and booze he had won in pub quiz contests. He was clutching a giant box of liqueur chocolates. Dick did not really believe that the seer could give him useful information about the Campbells or Beryl

Shuttleworth, but he still longed for Shona—Shona who was also called Macdonald like the seer, surely a good omen.

The seer's cottage was on top of a steep brae and Dick felt quite breathless when he pulled at the old-fashioned tirling pin on the door.

Angus opened the door. He was a tall bearded man, dressed in a long white robe like a Druid.

He accepted the liqueur chocolates and ushered Dick into his sitting room, which was lit by two oil lamps. Although Angus had electricity, he liked to keep the living room looking as antique as possible, from the blackened kettle hung over the peat fire to the large old-fashioned dresser against one wall.

Angus settled himself in an armchair on one side of the fire, and Dick sat down opposite on a high-backed Orkney chair. "How can I help you?" asked Angus.

Dick took a deep breath "I'm keen on this girl at the library, Shona Macdonald. She's a lot younger than I am. Do you think I have any hope there?"

"You havenae a hope in hell," said Angus. "Her heart belongs to another."

"How do you know that?"

"The spirits tell me," said Angus sententiously, who had actually read about Shona's engagement in the *Highland Times* that morning.

"She would ha' told me!" exclaimed Dick.

"She never even thought of you romantically," said the seer. "You're too auld."

"And you're a daft silly old man," said Dick wrathfully.

He got to his feet and strode to the door. "Tell Hamish Macbeth to look out for her," called the seer.

Dick swung round. "Who? What woman?"

"I don't know yet."

"Stupid fraud," muttered Dick and went out and slammed the door.

By the time he got back down to the police station, the rain Hamish had forecast was driving in horizontal sheets.

Hamish was sitting at the table reading the *Highland Times*. He looked at Dick's distressed face, got up, took a bottle of whisky out of a cupboard, and poured him a dram. "What did he say to upset you?"

"He said Shona, that girl at the library, is engaged. He said the spirits told him."

Hamish flipped the newspaper to the announcements and then silently handed it to Dick. He read that Shona was engaged to a man called Diarmuid Hendry.

In a funny kind of way, Dick felt a slow feeling almost of relief. His feelings for Shona had been growing into an obsession.

"I'd better get her an engagement present," he said.

"Look in your cupboard," said Hamish. "There's a spare toaster there."

Dick was about to protest that it should be something really special, but then he realised that a simple gift would do—a not-so-special gift from a not-so-special man.

"They're draining that bog tomorrow," said Hamish. "Want to come and have a look?"

"Maybe I'll take the toaster or something over to Shona."

"Wrap it up and post it," said Hamish gently.

"All right. I'll do that."

By the next morning, the rain had stopped and a pale disk of a sun shone down on the cold countryside, where water dripped from the few trees and the air was full of the smell of peat smoke.

Dick loaded the inevitable picnic hamper into the back of the Land Rover, along with water and food bowls for the dog and cat.

Sonsie and Lugs now travelled in the passenger seat with Dick, Sonsie on his lap and the dog at his feet.

"Put the beasts in the back," said Hamish.

"They don't bother me," said Dick placidly. "Sonsie's like a fur rug and Lugs keeps my feet warm."

When they arrived at the bog, the water was being drained off and a JCB stood ready to dig.

Jimmy stood at the edge of the bog, huddled in an anorak. "No Blair?" asked Hamish.

"He says it's a waste o' time."

"Is there any connection between Murdo and Beryl Shuttleworth?" asked Hamish.

"Nothing that we can see. She says labour is hard to come by and she didn't dig into the background of the

Campbell brothers. Andy has a record but it's only drunk and disorderly."

Dick had opened the back of the Land Rover and was pulling out a picnic table and three canvas chairs.

"I see wifie ower there is well prepared," said Jimmy.

Hamish scowled. If only Dick would fall in love with someone nearer his age and get settled, then he could get his home back again all to himself.

"Food's ready," called Dick. "I brought some for you, Mr. Anderson."

They took their places at the table. Dick served up salmon steaks and salad with rolls he had baked. The dog and cat, on the heather at their feet, ate chopped lamb's liver.

To Jimmy's delight, Dick also had a bottle of Sancerre which he poured into crystal glasses.

"I tell you, Dick," said Jimmy, raising his glass, "if Hamish ever throws you out, you can move in wi' me."

Elspeth Grant got an urgent call on her road north from Barry Dalrymple, the head of the news department. "There's a report come in that they're digging up some bog near the Seven Steps restaurant. Get over there instead."

By the time Elspeth arrived, a group of press had already assembled. She went to join Hamish.

"What's going on?" she asked.

"Just seeing if there are any bodies in there," said Hamish. "Like who?"

"Like I'm not telling you until it's official—that is, if they do find anyone."

Hamish looked down at her and felt a pang of longing. They had been engaged but that had broken up. I've been engaged to two women and it all came to nothing, he thought. Priscilla was too cold and Elspeth here went right off after we were engaged and had a fling with a male stripper.

Elspeth had got drunk down in Glasgow after having seen Hamish and Priscilla on camera, laughing and talking together. But although she had gone off with the male stripper, nothing had happened.

They stood together in silence and watched the digging.

Hamish left Elspeth and joined Jimmy. "Aren't they being a bittie brutal shovelling away like that?"

"It's not Richard the Third," said Jimmy. "And it's not an archaeological dig. And it's bloody freezing. Let them get on with it before some tree huggers turn up and tell us we're destroying the habitat of the red-breasted pushover or something."

Night falls early in the winter in Sutherland. Arc lights were set up, and the digging went on. Up came some skeletons but they were of first a deer, and then a cat and dog. Other things like a supermarket trolley and an old fridge followed.

"Come away from the lights, over here!" called Dick suddenly.

Jimmy and Hamish rushed to join him.

"What?" asked Hamish.

"Look at the sky!"

They looked up. Above them the northern lights blazed and undulated and swam across the sky in all their green glory. Living so far north, Hamish had seen the aurora borealis before, but never such a fine spectacle as this.

Elspeth joined them and then the other members of the press.

Hamish glanced back to where the arc light shone down on the bog. The digger was lifting up another shovelful of earth when Hamish saw a leg dangling from the shovel.

"Hold it right there!" he called, running forward.

Plastic sheets were spread out, and the contents of the shovel tipped out onto them.

A peat bog is a great preserver. The body looked intact, but they had to wait for the pathologist.

A tent was erected over the body, which was covered in black mud from the bog.

Hamish paced up and down impatiently. Blair appeared on the scene. He glared at Hamish. "Get back to your station. There are enough of us here, laddie."

"It was Macbeth's idea that there might be a body in the bog," said Daviot's voice behind Blair. "He stays."

"Right, sir. Anything you say, sir," grovelled Blair.

At last, Daviot was called forward. He bent down and went into the tent. After a few minutes he came out again and went up to Hamish. "I recognise him. It's that fellow Gonzales."

"We're still looking for thae Campbell brithers," said Blair. "Should we keep digging?"

"I don't think they're in there," said Hamish. "There's every evidence that they committed the murder."

Hamish drew Jimmy aside. "How many people have been charged with the trafficking?"

"Do you mean drugs or prostitutes?"

"Both."

"It's about over a hundred, and that includes the harbour master down at the docks. He's screaming that he knew nothing about it, but, man, you should see his bank balance. He must have been taking hefty bribes."

"Will I be needed when it gets to the High Court?"

"No, Hamish, we've got enough people to testify."

"And enough to take the glory."

"Aw, c'mon. You like to keep a low profile in case you're promoted."

"Yes, but I can't help wondering why I never get a thank-you. How was Gonzales killed?"

"Wait a minute." Jimmy walked over to Daviot. After a few minutes he came back to Hamish. "A blow to the back of the head that crushed his skull."

When Hamish returned to the station, he wondered again about Beryl and the Campbell brothers.

It was such a loose end, and Strathbane would be too occupied in all the paperwork necessary to bring so many to justice. He decided to call on Beryl the following evening.

* * *

Hetty stared sourly at Shona's diamond engagement ring. "The stone's not very big," she said.

"It's a very fine diamond," said Shona defensively. "You have to pay for quality."

"Men!" Hetty gave a shrill laugh. "Is that what he told you? Anyway, I'm thinking I might get married myself."

"Who to?"

"I think that little policeman, Dick, rather fancies me."

Chapter Nine

☠

By the pricking of my thumbs,
Something wicked this way comes.
                                    —William Shakespeare

Hamish drove up to Beryl's villa the following evening. She opened the door to him and looked in surprise at his well-tailored suit, white silk shirt, and tie.

"Why are you all dressed up?" she asked.

"I was hoping to take you to dinner. I have questions to ask you but I never called to welcome you to the area so this is a way of doing both."

She hesitated a moment and then shrugged. "Why not?"

Hamish drove them to the Tommel Castle Hotel. He thought briefly of his dwindling bank balance and found himself hoping she was guilty of something so that he could charge the dinner on his expenses.

When they were seated at a corner table, Beryl eyed

Hamish with some amusement. "I didn't think a mere police sergeant could afford clothes like the ones you've got on."

"There is a verra good thrift shop in Strathbane," said Hamish.

To his relief, Beryl said she would stick to the set menu. She looked round the dining room. "Quiet tonight," she commented. "The press must have given up."

"They cannae report much until all the trials," said Hamish.

The first course of venison pâté arrived. "What did you want to ask me?" said Beryl.

"I want to ask you again if you had any business dealings with Murdo Bentley?"

"That would make me a crook."

"I didn't mean that. I am sure he put some money into legitimate businesses."

"No, all my own work. My husband was an estate agent in Ripon in Yorkshire. He died of cancer and left me the business. I wanted a change and the idea of the Highlands had always attracted me. So I sold up, came up to Strathbane first of all, bought some properties, and did them up for rental. But Strathbane is a dismal place so I decided to move here."

"It can get rough in the winter."

"So can Yorkshire," said Beryl. "Maybe worse than here because you're near the Gulf Stream. Now shut up for a bit and let me eat."

Hamish waited patiently. The second course of fresh

trout with sautéed potatoes arrived. She filleted her fish with the neat dexterity of a surgeon. "The food here is delicious."

"Clarry, the chef," said Hamish, "used to work for me as a police officer. He was a lousy policeman but a great cook so he changed jobs."

He waited until she had finished and asked, "Tell me your impressions of the Campbell brothers?"

Those unfathomable black eyes of hers stared at him for a moment from under her hooded lids. Then she said, "Rough and ready. Good odd-job men. Did repairs. Cleaned gutters. Tidied up gardens. Things like that. I can't tell you anything else. It's not as if I socialised with them."

Hamish found himself wishing Beryl was innocent of any crime. Although not precisely good looking, she exuded a strong air of sensuality and femininity. She was wearing a dress of soft green wool which clung to the curves of her figure, and her perfume smelt of roses.

Hamish reminded himself that a long stretch of celibacy could prove dangerous.

She stared at him over a generous dessert of chocolate cake soaked in Armagnac and covered in whipped cream. "Stop taking inventory of the goods," she said. "What is the result? Are you wondering what I would be like in bed or whether I am capable of murder?"

"Both," said Hamish. "And the one cancels out the other."

"Pity."

The waiter approached and put a foil-wrapped parcel on the table. "The usual from the chef," he said.

Hamish thanked him. Beryl looked amused. "Is that another dinner for you?"

"No. I have a dog and a cat, and Clarry often gives me scraps for them."

"I bet if anything happened to your pets it would be like losing children."

"Something like that."

Hamish took out his notebook. He had an iPad but still carried a small notebook around with him. "Let me see," he said. "The Campbell brothers used to live in a council flat over at Bonar Bridge before they moved into one of your cottages at Burn Brae just outside Strathbane."

"Which had to be cleaned because the previous renters were pigs."

"They were Scottish, weren't they? The Campbells?"

"As haggis."

"As far as you know, these are their correct names?"

"How could I know any different?"

"You were their employer. They would have given you proof of identity."

"Look, Hamish. I told you. It's hard to get help. I paid them cash out of the business account and it was up to them to pay tax on it. Are you going to arrest me?"

"If I arrested everyone who was paying someone off the books in the Highlands, I'd need to book half the population," said Hamish. "Did either of them have a wife or girlfriend?"

She waited until the waiter had poured their coffee. "Not that I know of."

"There is no record of either of them having a bank account or credit cards."

"I wouldn't worry about it," she said. "They're probably long gone."

"On one of the CCTV tapes from the restaurant, Murdo is shown stopping at your table to talk to you and yet you say you barely knew him."

"Murdo liked to play the squire. He always stopped at a lot of tables. Asked me how business was going, that sort of thing."

"And how is business? Can't be any tourists at this time of year."

"If I relied on the tourists, I'd go broke. I rent to students from the university and people from the electronics firm. I reduce the rental for long lets because it saves on cleaning and changing linen."

Beryl finished her coffee. "Now, if you've stopped grilling me, I'd like to get to bed."

He drove her to her villa and walked her to her door. "Thank you for dinner," she said. She stood on tiptoe and kissed him full on the mouth. For one brief moment, Hamish responded, and then he pushed her gently away.

He got into his Land Rover and drove down the short

drive to find the entrance blocked by a car. The barman from the hotel got out.

"Mr. Macbeth," he said, "there's a copper frae Strathbane breathalysing all the folk arriving or leaving."

"I'll park the Land Rover here, Paul," said Hamish. "Give me a lift back to the hotel. I'd like to see who this copper is."

When Hamish arrived in the car park, Colonel Halburton-Smythe, the owner, was complaining to a policeman Hamish did not recognise.

"Harassing my guests," the colonel was shouting. "I'll complain to your superior officer."

"Leave it to me, Colonel," said Hamish. He said to the policeman, "You're on my beat. Who sent you here?"

"Detective Chief Inspector Blair," he replied. He was a burly officer with a great round face and small piggy eyes. "He said there had been bad reports."

"Wait there," said Hamish. "Go inside, Colonel. I'll get to the bottom of this."

He took out his mobile phone, checked his contacts, and phoned Superintendent Daviot at home.

Daviot listened to Hamish's complaint. Hamish ended by saying, "Remember what happened to the last policeman that Blair sent to snoop around."

"But didn't Mr. Blair contact you?"

"No, he did not. And Colonel Halburton-Smythe is thinking of suing you for harassment."

"Put the officer on the phone."

Hamish handed the phone to the policeman. He listened in glee to the "yes, sirs" and "only following orders, sir."

The policeman gloomily handed the phone back to Hamish. "I will call Colonel Halburton-Smythe right away," said Daviot. "I am afraid Mr. Blair is overzealous. What is the name of the policeman?"

"Name?" asked Hamish turning to the officer.

"Bert McAlpine."

Hamish told Daviot the name. "Tell him to tear up any charges," ordered Daviot.

He was about to leave and walk back to his vehicle when Hamish saw a television van parked near the entrance. He walked to the window of the bar and looked in. Elspeth was sitting with two men and a girl. He hurried in.

Elspeth gave him a rather bleak welcome. "Can we talk?" asked Hamish.

She rose reluctantly to her feet. He followed her into the hotel lounge where she sat down in an armchair by the window. Hamish sat opposite her. She looked at him accusingly, and a stuffed stag's head on the wall of the lounge seemed to mimic her stare.

"What?"

"Did you file a story?"

"The body in the bog, yes. My researcher did some background on Eriskay for me. She did various interviews with the islanders. Martha was regarded as a harmless eccentric. I saw you in the dining room earlier but you were romancing some female as usual."

"Thon woman is a suspect as far as I am concerned, that's all."

"Do you buy all your suspects expensive dinners?"

"C'mon, Elspeth. No one else suspects her so it was my way of finding out more about her."

"The barman said you were snogging her."

"She was kissing me and what the hell has it to do with you?"

Elspeth half rose from her seat and then sank down again with a reluctant laugh.

"Tell me all about it, Hamish. You always did need a Watson."

There was no one like Elspeth, thought Hamish; Elspeth with her silvery Gypsy eyes and her odd psychic way of seeing things other people missed.

He talked about finding Gonzales's body in the bog, about how the Campbell brothers were suspected of murdering him and how Beryl Shuttleworth had employed the pair.

"Maybe I'll go and interview her tomorrow morning," said Elspeth.

"Catch her before she goes to work," said Hamish. "Now, there's a framed photograph on her desk. When I was there it had been laid flat. See if you can get a look at it and tell me who's in the picture."

"I'll try. How's Priscilla?"

"In London as far as I know," said Hamish curtly. "How's Barry?"

"The same."

Elspeth had once been engaged to her boss until they both decided they were not suited to each other.

She rose to her feet. "I'm tired. I'll call you tomorrow. Give me Beryl's address and tell me how to get there."

When Hamish entered the police station kitchen, he found Hetty seated at the table with Dick, who flashed him a look of appeal.

"We have urgent business, Dick," said Hamish. "There's no time for you to put on your uniform. Hetty, I'm afraid you'll have to go."

Hetty stood up, then leaned forward and kissed Dick on the cheek. "Good night, lover boy," she said. "I'll be seeing you."

Hamish opened the door for her and saw her out into the night. He stood there until he was sure she had driven off before returning to the kitchen.

"What was that all about?" asked Hamish. "You looked like a rat caught in a trap."

"That's how I felt," said Dick. "She seems to think I'm keen on her. We shouldn't have let her drive. She's been drinking. I told her we hadn't any booze and gave her strong coffee. I tried again to get out of her something useful about Cyril but all I got was a load of bollocks about how some man who fancied her must have got jealous. How Shona can bear to work with her is beyond me."

"Maybe because she isn't trying her charms on Shona."

"How did you get on?"

"I've a feeling Beryl is stonewalling me. Elspeth is going to see her tomorrow."

That's all I need, thought Dick miserably, Hamish and Elspeth getting close again. He wished some dramatic news story would break and Elspeth would be called back to Glasgow.

"I'm off to bed," said Hamish. "Let's hope Elspeth comes up with something."

Hamish lay awake in his bed for a long while. He missed the cat and dog, who used to sleep with him and had now transferred their affections to Dick. If only, thought Hamish, his engagement to Elspeth had worked out. He would be sharing his home with a wife instead of a policeman.

Elspeth, with her crew of soundman, cameraman, and researcher, arrived on Beryl's doorstep at seven thirty in the morning. She opened the door to them wearing a dressing gown of patterned silk over a nightdress and blinked at them blearily.

"I wanted to interview you about the Campbell brothers," said Elspeth after introducing herself and her crew.

Beryl hesitated only a few minutes. She thought she might film well. "You'll need to wait until I get dressed," she said.

"May we come in?" asked Elspeth. "It's freezing out here."

"Can't you wait in that van of yours?"

"The heating won't work," lied Elspeth. "We're going to get the radiator checked. And we need to set up the lights and camera."

"Oh, all right. Come in."

Beryl left them in the living room and went off to get dressed.

While the lighting was being fixed and the camera got ready, Elspeth looked at the desk. No sign of a photograph. She slid open the top drawer. There was a framed photograph, facedown. She quickly turned it over. Beryl was standing in the middle. A couple had their arms round her. Elspeth recognised Murdo and Anna from photographs she had seen in the newspapers. They were standing on the terrace somewhere overlooking a view of palm trees and blue sea.

She slid the drawer shut and moved away from the desk. She felt a frisson of fear. If Beryl was pally with that villainous pair, then she was probably involved in their shady dealings.

Hamish had better look out.

Beryl was gone for half an hour. When she finally entered the living room, she was wearing a power suit with a very short skirt over a low-cut silk blouse. Elspeth felt a stab of jealousy. Beryl had very long legs encased in sheer black stockings. I'll bet it was Hamish who kissed her, she thought.

Elspeth began the questioning. Beryl told her pretty

much what she had told Hamish. Highlanders are champion liars, and Elspeth was no exception. She studied her notes and then said, "You claim that Murdo Bentley was only an acquaintance, someone you spoke to when you visited his restaurant, but that was all."

"Right."

"We have an informant who says you often travelled abroad with both Murdo Bentley and Anna Eskdale and stayed at the same hotels."

"Rubbish! Lies!" An ugly flush rose to Beryl's cheeks. "I've got to get to work so pack up your gear and go!"

"So you deny having a close relationship with them?" pursued Elspeth.

Beryl rose to her feet. "Get out!"

Everything was packed up. Elspeth was the last to leave. Beryl seized her by the arm and whispered, "Go carefully, *dear*, accidents do happen."

Elspeth borrowed a hotel car and drove down to the police station later that morning. She was about to sit down at the kitchen table when Dick said fussily, "Come through to the living room. The fire's lit and it's nice and cosy."

Elspeth looked at Dick, and Dick looked back. Why didn't I notice before? wondered Elspeth. I've got an enemy here. Why? Does he fancy Hamish? No, it's not that. She looked around the living room, at the large flat-screen television and the bright slipcovers on the sofa and armchairs, at the little nest of polished tables, and at the fire burning brightly on the clean hearth. It's what he thinks of as *his* home, realised Elspeth, and he sees me as a threat.

Dick bustled off to fetch coffee. "So," said Hamish. "How did it go?"

Elspeth told him about the interview. Hamish's hazel eyes gleamed. "So she did know them! I wish you hadn't been lying, Elspeth. I'd like to get my hands on that photograph and confront her with it."

"Can't you get a search warrant?"

"I can try."

Dick came in with a tray of coffee and then returned with a plate of warm scones. "Try one of these," he urged. "I got the recipe from the Currie sisters."

Elspeth wanted to say, *I don't want your scones. I think somehow you buggered up my engagement,* but she meekly thanked him instead.

Hamish went off to the office to phone Strathbane. He phoned directly to Daviot. To his surprise, Daviot agreed to the search warrant, Hamish momentarily forgetting that a grateful boss would pretty much have granted him anything. He then phoned Jimmy, who agreed to get a squad ready. They planned to go to her home that evening.

Hamish then returned to the living room and told them about his success. "Don't film it, Elspeth," he urged. "If there's nothing there, we'll look like fools."

Hamish tried to concentrate on paperwork involving minor cases for the rest of the day, but he felt too tensed up to do the work properly. The raid was planned for eight o'clock that evening. An unmarked police car would follow Beryl when she finished work to make sure she was going home.

At last, it was time. Hamish and Dick waited a little way off from the villa for the others to arrive.

When they did come, he was surprised not to see the truculent form of Blair with his bloated whisky face emerging from one of the cars.

"Where's Blair?" he asked Jimmy.

"Said he had something else to do."

Hamish felt a pang of unease. What if there were an informant in the police force and Blair somehow knew Beryl had been tipped off?

Jimmy led the way up to the door and rang the bell. In that moment, Hamish found himself wishing that Jimmy didn't smell so strongly of whisky pretty much all the time. One of these days, Jimmy's evidence would be thrown out of court, the accused claiming the detective was drunk.

Beryl opened the door and faced them. Hamish's heart sank to his regulation boots. She looked completely unfazed when Jimmy told her about the search warrant.

"You're wasting your time," she said calmly.

"This policewoman will escort you to wait in a car," said Jimmy.

Beryl shrugged and walked off with the policewoman.

When the search began, Hamish went straight to the desk. There was no photograph on it or in it. He turned round and looked at the living room. It smelt strongly of polish and cleaning fluid. He suddenly felt sure it was no use searching for anything incriminating. But he searched the whole desk and the underside of the drawers without finding anything sinister.

The villa was searched from top to bottom without finding anything incriminating. "Now you've landed us in it," muttered Jimmy fiercely.

Beryl surveyed them calmly as she got out of the police car. "You will be hearing from my lawyers," she said. She looked straight at Hamish. "I am disappointed in you," she added and marched off into her house.

"I'm telling you," said Hamish. "She got a tip-off."

"Och, get back tae your sheep," said Jimmy disgustedly. "As the senior officer, I'll be the one to get the flak."

Hamish drove Dick to the police station. "I'm off on a call, Dick. I don't want you to come with me in case I land in trouble."

Hamish drove straight to Strathbane. Frost on the grass at the side of the road glittered in his headlamps, and the pitiless stars of Sutherland blazed overhead.

He braked suddenly as a suicidal sheep ambled onto the road. "Get the hell out o' it!" he roared out of the window, taking out his worry and pent-up fury on the sheep. It gave him a huffy look and with maddening slowness walked into the fields at the side of the road.

He drove near the Blairs' home and phoned. Blair's wife, Mary, answered.

"Is your man at home?" asked Hamish.

"No, he's in the pub as usual."

"I need to talk to you, Mary."

"I cannae see you here. Meet me in the bar of the Scotsman Hotel in town."

"Right."

Mary had been a prostitute that Hamish had once manipulated Blair into marrying. She had turned out an excellent wife for the boozy detective and had become a pillar of the community.

To Hamish's relief, the bar was quiet. Mary came in and sat down, looking at him anxiously. "What's he been up to now?" she asked.

The waitress came over. Mary ordered whisky and Hamish, a tonic water. When the drinks were served, Hamish leaned forward and said urgently, "Has your man had more money than he should have had in the past months?"

Her eyes widened. "D'ye mean, is he on the take?"

"Something like that." Hamish told her about the useless search, ending by saying, "I'm sure she was tipped off."

She shook her head. "I handle all the money and pay all the bills. I have to or he would drink us broke. What gives you that idea?"

"First he put Cyril on to spy on me, next he gets another one, Bert McAlpine, to breathalyse folk at the Tommel Castle Hotel where I had been having dinner. He maybe hoped to get me on a drunk driving charge. So maybe the tip-off wasn't for money but to make me look like a fool. Did he know Murdo Bentley?"

"Just at the restaurant. We had a couple of free meals there. I protested but he said everyone did it. Look, Hamish, I don't want him getting into trouble. I have a comfy life and I handle him just grand."

"I'll do my best. It would be better if someone like me found out than, say, Jimmy. How's life anyway?"

"Great. Me and Mrs. Daviot are bosom buddies." Mary giggled. "She'd die if she ever found out about me."

"She won't," said Hamish, surveying the plump woman with the grey hair and well-cut tweeds. "You look the picture of respectability."

Hamish drove back to Lochdubh, but on an impulse he drove near Beryl's villa and parked down the road.

He took off his regulation cap and pulled on a black wool one to hide his red hair. He walked to the villa and hid in the rhododendron bushes in the drive. The curtains on the windows of the living room were opened. As he watched, Beryl walked to the window and looked out. Then she turned around and could be seen talking to someone. Who?

Hamish knew he could not get close to the windows because there were no concealing bushes in front of them and his boots would make a noise on the gravel. He shivered. The night was cold. He was only wearing his regulation sweater over a shirt and trousers. He had left his coat in the car.

An owl swooped overhead, making him jump. Somewhere a rabbit squealed in its death throes. Probably caught by a ferret. The fauna of the highland countryside was settling down to its business of massacring the weakest.

People who said they didn't believe in God often said, "But I worship nature." And that, thought Hamish, was about as safe as worshipping the old Greek gods. Climbers, unaware of the perils of the weather, were regularly killed, inexperienced yachtsmen blown to kingdom come on the crosswinds on some loch. His thoughts were interrupted by the sound of a car arriving. A taxi swept up the drive and stopped at the door.

The front door opened and Blair came out, followed by Beryl. "Go safely," she called, waving goodbye.

Blair settled back in the taxi on the road to Strathbane. There was no better feeling than landing Hamish Macbeth in the shit. Fine woman, that Beryl.

"There's a police car coming up behind us," called the taxi driver. "He's flashing his lights for me to pull over."

"Do it," ordered Blair.

The cab door was jerked open and Hamish Macbeth said, "Get out now."

"How dare you order me around," blustered Blair.

"Do you want this taxi driver to hear exactly why I'm ordering you around? Tell him to wait."

Blair sulkily gave instructions to the driver. "Get in the Land Rover," ordered Hamish.

When Blair was seated in the passenger seat, Hamish said, "Did you tip off Beryl that there was going to be a house search?"

"Bollocks," yelled Blair. "She was upset about the search and Mr. Daviot suggested I pay a courtesy call."

"I have Mr. Daviot's home number," said Hamish. "I'll just call and confirm that."

He took out his mobile and began to dial.

"Wait!" shouted Blair. "Look, laddie, the truth is I did it off ma ain bat. There was nothing to link her to any wrongdoing, and I thocht the search was a bad mistake."

"The reason for the search, as you should know," said Hamish, "was because we had enough on her to warrant a search. I'll just make that call."

"No! Look. Okay, I know the wumman. You know they've closed down the police accommodation. Well, occasionally she lets out cottages to coppers at a damn reasonable price."

"I still should report you," said Hamish.

"What more do you want?" shouted Blair.

"For a start, what did you have on Cyril Sessions to get him to agree to spy on me? Had he not been murdered, he would have lost his job. I know you didn't lose yours, God knows why. Out with it."

"He was visiting this prostitute and not paying her for

giving him a leg over. She'd had enough and was going to report him. I shut her up."

"Name of prostitute."

"I dinnae call tae mind."

"I call to mind Daviot's phone number."

"Oh, all right. It's Betty Blue."

"Real name?"

"Betty Queen."

"Address?"

"Number Five, Cockspur Street."

"Is it a brothel?"

"Naw, she's upmarket. Got a house of her own."

"Prostitutes are often tied up to criminals. Did you never think that might be behind the murder of Cyril?"

"Sessions must have been doing something for Bentley. That lot killed him."

"Just before she died, Anna Eskdale said they didn't."

"Probably didnae know she was going to die. Lying."

"I've a feeling we'll soon get enough to arrest Beryl," said Hamish. "If I find she's fled, then I'm going to talk about you. Get along with you and don't sic anyone on me again!"

Hamish watched Blair walk back to his cab. If it wasn't for his wife, he thought, I'd report the old bastard like a shot.

At the police station, Dick said, "Elspeth called to say she wouldn't be hanging around."

Hamish went into the office and phoned Elspeth. "Dick tells me you phoned to say you were leaving?"

"I didn't call at all," said Elspeth.

"Why on earth did he say so?"

"He looks on me as a rival."

"Come off it, Elspeth."

"He thinks if we got together again, he'd be out of his precious home, scones, chintz slipcovers, the lot."

"I don't want to talk about it," said Hamish.

"You never did want to talk about anything important," said Elspeth and banged down the phone.

Hamish went back to the living room. "You made that up," he said to Dick. "Why?"

"She's not right for you," said Dick.

"All you care about," said Hamish nastily, "is playing housewife in my station. I'm going to get you sent back to Strathbane."

He slammed out of the room, leaving Dick to hug the cat and look mournfully round what he thought of as his little palace.

In the morning, Hamish curtly refused Dick's offer of breakfast, called to the dog and cat, and went out to the Land Rover.

As he drove out of Lochdubh, he saw Hetty behind the wheel of her car, heading for the police station. Before that business about Elspeth, he would have phoned Dick to warn him, but he was still feeling bitter.

Dick was sitting at the kitchen table, reading the *Highland Times*, when Hetty walked in.

"What are you doing here?" he cried.

Hetty smiled roguishly at him, "I came to see you, silly."

"I'm just off on an important case," said Dick. "Shouldn't you be at the library?"

"It's Sunday! I thought, I'll just run over and see my dear Dick."

Dick could feel sweat trickling down the back of his neck. He walked straight to the kitchen door and held it open for her. "Sorry, I've got to go. Got to get my uniform on." He turned away and went into his bedroom.

When he came out, he saw the kitchen door was still open. He was about to leave in case she was still waiting out on the road when he heard a faint noise from the living room.

He went in and found Hetty wandering around, looking at everything.

"You can't stay here!" said Dick. "Please leave."

"It's really cosy here," said Hetty. "But you need a wife to give it the feminine touch."

"Out! Now!" said Dick. "I've got to lock up."

Hetty moved slowly to the door. She moved up close to him, and he backed away.

"So shy," she whispered. "But I'll change all that."

Dick sidestepped her. "I'll be back," she said, like some horrible travesty of Arnold Schwarzenegger.

Dick mopped his brow after she had left. The woman was obsessed. And so are you, said the voice of his conscience. Hamish will never forgive you, and all because you're so in love with a police station, you interfered in his engagement.

Hamish parked in front of the address in Cockspur Street. Betty Queen lived in a small bungalow on the outskirts of Strathbane.

He went up and rang the bell. "Is Miss Queen at home?" he asked the small, motherly woman who answered the door.

"I am Betty Queen. What do you want?"

"Just a wee chat," said Hamish.

"All right. Come in."

Hamish reflected that her living room would have delighted Dick. It was clean and comfortable, and the delicious smell of something cooking came from the kitchen. He looked curiously at Betty. She was plump with a round rosy face and brown hair. Her only claim to beauty was a pair of excellent legs.

"How did you get into the life?" he asked curiously.

"My husband deserted me, leaving me with a baby girl. I needed money and I had no skills. I was being interviewed for a job as a housekeeper in the bar of the Scotsman Hotel. The woman who was interviewing me said she could not take on a woman with a child and left. I was about to leave when this businessman came up and offered me a drink. I felt I needed a drink and one thing led to another. He began to pay me for services rendered and gave me gifts. Everything was fine until he said he was being moved on, that is, with his wife and family. So I went back to the hotel, picked up another one, and then began to advertise in the Internet."

"You advertised prostitution! It's a miracle the police didn't close you down."

"I advertised home comforts for weary businessmen. A lot of them are frightened of the lovelies imported from Eastern Europe. My daughter's at Cambridge. Before that, I was able to send her to a good boarding school. Are you here to arrest me?"

"No. I'm here to ask you about Cyril Sessions."

Her small nose wrinkled in disgust. "If we're going to talk about him, I need some coffee. Wait there."

After some time, she came back with the coffee things and a plate of oatcakes spread with cream cheese. "I baked the oatcakes, and the cheese is from Orkney. Help yourself.

"Now, Cyril was a monster. He wanted freebies and said if I didn't give him what he wanted, he would report me. I hated him. At last, I phoned the police to report him and some great fat detective called on me. He said if I left Cyril alone then he would make sure Cyril left me alone, and that was the last I saw of Cyril."

"So what did he talk about? These oatcakes are great." Hamish was about to ask for the recipe to give to Dick and then remembered he wanted nothing more to do with the man.

"Help yourself. I've lots more. Cyril bragged a lot. He hinted that he was soon going to be rich. He said he had the goods on someone. As he was already blackmailing me, I assume he had found someone else to put the screws on."

"Do you know if that someone was Murdo Bentley?"

"The racketeer. I read about him in the newspapers. I assumed that was why Cyril was murdered. Why are you staring at me like that?"

"Did you never think of getting married?"

"Well, it would be nice, wouldn't it? I've thought about it lately. I've enough in the bank and I'm thinking of retiring."

"Do your neighbours know you're on the game?"

"There's no one close by. I go to the kirk on Sundays. They think I'm respectable."

"If you can think of anything more that might be useful, here is my card. I wonder if I could take some of your baking back with me. I'll gladly pay you."

"Don't be silly. I'm flattered. Do you know? Talking to you has cheered me up. You look at me as if I'm a real woman. I think I will retire. Wait and I'll make you up a box."

Hamish dropped the box on the kitchen table at the police station and said mildly, "I had to go to headquarters about something and I called in on an old friend o' mine. She's a champion baker."

Relieved that Hamish was talking to him, Dick opened the box. It contained two plastic containers. One held the oatcakes and another, chocolate muffins.

Dick bit into an oatcake and then raised his eyes. "Man,

there are oatcakes and oatcakes but these come straight from heaven. Did you get the recipe?"

"You know what these champion cooks are like," said Hamish. "We've got a quiet day. Here's her address. She's called Betty Queen. Why don't you call on her?"

Dick tried a bit of chocolate muffin. "I've just got to find out how she does it."

"Don't put your uniform on," said Hamish. "She might think there's a death in the family when she opens the door."

Betty looked curiously at the small figure of Dick on her doorstep. "I'm a friend of Hamish's," said Dick.

"You'd better come in," said Betty sadly. She thought that Hamish had sent along one of his friends as a client.

When they were seated in the living room, she said, "And what can I do for you?" She hoped it was nothing kinky.

Dick's eyes shone with an almost religious fervour. "It's your baking," he said. "Hamish told me you were a champion baker. I'm good myself, but you're a genius. Is there any hope of a recipe?"

Betty's face lit up. "Come through to the kitchen and I'll show you how I do it."

After three hours of cooking lessons, Dick looked at his watch. "It's getting late. Tell you what, there's a grand Italian restaurant over in Lochdubh. Why don't I take you there for dinner?"

She smiled at him. "That would be grand."

* * *

Hamish was strolling along the waterfront with his dog and cat when he saw Dick and Betty seated at a table in the window of the Italian restaurant. He turned to go back to the police station when he saw Hetty's car coming along the waterfront.

He went straight into the restaurant. "Move to a table at the back," he said to Dick. "Evening, Betty. Some woman is pursuing Dick and if she sees you, she'll join you. Give me your car keys and I'll move it."

"Hetty?" asked Dick.

"The same."

"Let's move, Betty," said Dick urgently. "I'll tell you all about it."

After driving Dick's car round to the back of the restaurant, Hamish returned his keys and then went back out and strolled towards the police station. Hetty was sitting in her parked car. Hamish rapped on the window and she rolled down the glass.

"What are you doing here?" he demanded.

"I've come to see Dick."

"Constable Fraser is visiting his fiancée in Perth," said Hamish.

"But he said nothing to me about a fiancée!" exclaimed Hetty.

"Why should he?" demanded Hamish. "He wasn't dating you."

"He led me on!"

"Havers! Now, move along, lassie, or I'll book you for obstructing the entrance to a police station."

With a great savage grinding of gears, Hetty did a U-turn and sped off.

"So things are going well," said Hamish to Sonsie and Lugs. "But what the hell is going to happen when he finds out she's a prostitute?"

Over coffee, Betty said with a sigh, "I did enjoy that. Did Hamish tell you about me?"

"He said you were a champion baker. Why did he go to see you? I didnae ask."

"When I tell you, you won't want to see me again."

"You'd better let me know what it was about."

"My husband cleared off and left me with a small child to bring up. I had no skills. I started selling myself. Cyril Sessions discovered me and started blackmailing me for free favours. I reported him and some detective told me he wouldn't bother me again if I kept quiet. I'm retired. I did my business very quietly. My own daughter knows nothing about it. I boarded her out at an early age. She's at Cambridge now."

A fat tear rolled down her cheek. "And along you come and treat me like a lady and I've loved every minute of it."

She began to cry in earnest. Dick took out a large clean handkerchief and handed it to her.

He waited until she had recovered and then he said, "Have you seen the new James Bond movie?"

"No."

"Would you like to go tomorrow night?"

Betty stared at him in amazement. "You're asking me out on a date?"

"Another date. This is one."

"Oh, I would love to."

"It's showing here in the village hall tomorrow night at seven o' clock. I'll pick you up at six."

"I'm sorry I had to tell you about my life," said Betty.

"Let's forget about it."

When Dick returned to the police station, he said to Hamish, "You should ha' told me about her."

"She's retired," said Hamish. "I thought you would enjoy her baking, that's all."

"Well, don't tie me up the morrow night, I'm taking Betty to the pictures at the village hall. Did you manage to get rid of Hetty?"

"Yes. Have a word with Shona. I think something should be done about her. I think the woman is deranged."

"I'll take a run over tomorrow. What will you be doing?"

"I'm going to stalk Beryl. I feel sure she knows where the Campbell brothers are."

The following morning, Hamish phoned the Tommel Castle Hotel to be told that Elspeth had been called back to Glasgow.

He felt a pang of disappointment. He went along to Angela's and asked to borrow her car. He didn't want Beryl to see the police Land Rover.

Hamish found a parking place outside her rental office and settled down to wait. She had two girls working for her. He waited until he saw one of the girls leaving for her lunch hour, got out of the car, and followed her.

She went into a Burger King. Hamish stood behind her while she placed her order, then collected a container of coffee for himself and followed her to her table. Fortunately, the place was crowded. "May I join you?" he asked.

She nodded. She was small, just about five feet high, with brown hair streaked with blonde, a nose ring, and a spotty face.

"Cold day," ventured Hamish. "Might get snow."

"Jings!" she said. "That a fact?"

"Working hard?"

"Och, it's aye slow in the winter."

"Good boss?"

"Bitch frae hell, but jobs are hard to come by."

"I saw in the papers that the police were looking for a couple of men who used to work for her."

"Oh, them. That was afore my time. What do you do?"

"I'm a crofter," said Hamish.

"Sheep and a' that?"

"Yes. Healthy life."

"Wouldnae suit me. I'm going to be on telly one o' thae days."

"And how do you manage that?"

She looked at him coyly. "The Strathbane Telly folk hang out at the Scotsman. I go there some evenings with my pals. I saw one o' them looking at me. I'll be discovered."

Uncovered, more likely, in a hotel room and put down as an easy lay, thought Hamish cynically.

He realised she could not have any useful information. "Got to go," he said. "Sheep to see, people to do."

When he returned to his car, he suddenly felt he was wasting time. If Beryl had any contact with the brothers, it would be under cover of darkness.

Dick waited until he saw Shona leave for her lunch and followed her into the café.

"Why, Dick!" said Shona "Grand to see you."

Dick congratulated her on her engagement and then said, "We're getting right worried about Hetty. She's started stalking me and we're sure she's gone mad. Hamish suggests you have a word wi' the library board."

"I couldn't do that," said Shona. "I don't have any proof. I mean, in the library, she does her job just fine."

"Go carefully. She's beginning to scare me," said Dick.

They talked about Shona's forthcoming wedding, Dick finding to his amazement that now he just looked on her as a young friend.

* * *

The girl Hamish had met in Burger King was chatting about the crofter she had met at lunchtime. "He was asking about the Campbell brothers," she said.

"What did he look like?" asked Beryl.

"Great big loon wi' bright red hair."

"Get on with your work," snapped Beryl. She retreated to her inner office to make a phone call.

Chapter Ten

☠

I have no relish for the country; it is a kind of healthy grave.

—*Sydney Smith*

Two frustrating weeks went by for Hamish Macbeth. At night, he hid in the shrubbery at Beryl's place, hoping for some clue, without success.

Dick was out most evenings, visiting Betty and giving Hamish pangs of conscience. What hope did his romance have? If they were seen together and Betty recognised for what she was, or rather had been recently, then Dick would be in trouble.

Then Hamish got a call late one evening from Strathbane. A report of a burglary had come in. He was given an address of a cottage on the moors before Strathbane. He was told a Mrs. McLeigh had called for help. He asked Dick if he could use his car, as there was something up with the Land Rover. Deciding not to waste time putting on his uniform, he slipped a small tape recorder inside his pocket before he set off. He found its records useful when writing up his notes.

He arrived at the cottage. The door was standing open and light was streaming out over the heather.

Hamish entered cautiously. "Mrs. McLeigh," he called.

A heavy blow struck him on the back of the head and he slumped to the ground.

He slowly recovered consciousness some time later. He was feeling dizzy and sick, but some instinct told him to keep his eyes closed. A man's voice said, "Well, Andy, here we are at the bog, but it's still dug up."

The Campbell brothers at last, thought Hamish. He could tell that his wrists and feet were bound tightly because of the pain.

"Let's search him first," said what must be the other brother, Davy. "Maybe he's got some money on him."

"I saw a wallet in his back pocket. Roll him over," said Andy.

Hamish was thrust on his face. Then came Andy's shocked voice. "That bitch never told us it was the polis. She just said some fellow would arrive at the cottage, to knock him out and bury him in the bog. But to kill a polis!"

Came Davy's voice, "Aye but she's got our passports in that safe of hers. She said after this, she would let us have them and money to get abroad."

"This is Hamish Macbeth, him that's often in the papers. There'll be an international manhunt."

There was a long silence. Then Andy said, "We could leave him here, get back to Beryl's, make her open the safe, top her, and get the hell out o' the country. I tell you, murder this polis and she'll have her claws even deeper into us. She's promised to let us go time after time and nothing happened. Cut the polis loose and let's get the hell out o' here. He's still breathing. Let's hope he doesn't croak."

Hamish felt his bonds slashed. He lay very still until he heard the sound of a vehicle fading in the distance.

He rolled over and felt in his pockets. The tape recorder was still there and running. They had not even taken his mobile phone. He phoned Strathbane and rapidly told them the situation, asking them to get to Beryl's house as fast as possible and send a car to pick him up at the bog.

Beryl opened the door to the Campbell brothers. "All done?" she asked. "That was quick."

Andy went round behind her and seized her in a strong grip. "Get the ropes, Davy," he shouted.

Beryl fought and screamed but to no avail. Soon she was tied to a chair.

"Gie us the combination to the safe," said Davy.

"No!" said Beryl.

"Go ahead," said Davy to his brother.

Andy took a can of petrol, opened it, and splashed the

contents all over Beryl. Then he flicked open a lighter and held it up. "The combination, lassie, or you burn."

Beryl closed her eyes and gave them the combination.

They went through and opened the safe. They took out their passports and wads of money.

"This'll get us out o' the country," said Andy.

They returned to the living room and surveyed Beryl.

"What do we do with her?" asked Davy.

"This," said Andy. He flicked open the lighter and threw it onto Beryl's lap.

She went up like a torch. "Let's beat it," said Andy. "She screamed enough to wake the dead."

They walked out of the villa to be faced with a squad of armed police. They turned to run, but the villa was in flames.

"Get down on the ground," shouted a policeman through a megaphone, "or we'll shoot."

Hamish arrived in time to see them being led away. A fire engine came roaring up, and soon hoses were being played on the burning building.

Hamish approached Jimmy. "I've got what they said at the bog on tape. If they shut the safe behind them, you may find stuff in there that she hid when we searched the house."

"You'd better get to the hospital," said Jimmy. "You're as white as a sheet. If you've got bleeding from the brain, you'll be dead by the morning."

Hamish phoned Dick from the hospital the next morning and told him about his adventures.

"Nobody phoned me," said Dick. "Where's my car?"

"I'll get them to search for it."

"I'll come over with Betty and see you."

"Not Betty," said Hamish. "They'll be in to take a statement from me, and Blair might be hanging around."

"Oh, right."

What on earth was Dick going to do about Betty, wondered Hamish.

Jimmy called later and waited while a policeman took a full statement. Then he said, "The safe survived the fire. I'm waiting until forensics are finished."

"What are the Campbell brothers saying, if anything?" asked Hamish.

"Nothing so far. But it looks as if they burned the Shuttleworth woman to death."

"I think that one thought she was invincible," said Hamish. "She knew I was watching her and she would ha' been the first suspect."

The results of Hamish's tests were good. He was advised to spend another night in hospital before going back to Lochdubh. Dick arrived bearing newspapers and grapes.

"Something awfy bad has happened," said Dick. "I got a phone call from Blair. He saw me with Betty. He said he would keep his mouth shut provided I did a few jobs for him."

"Number one being spying on me," said Hamish. "Don't worry. I'll shut him up."

"I've been thinking, Hamish. I might quit the force and move down to Perth with Betty. I could get a job as a security guard."

"That would be a grand idea," said Hamish. "Does Betty know?"

"I haven't asked her yet."

"Well, good luck."

After he had left, Hamish phoned Blair. "If you talk about Betty's history," he said, "then much as I admire and like your wife, her background story will be all over the newspapers and I will tell Daviot how you tipped Beryl off about the search." Blair cursed and ranted but finally agreed to keep his mouth shut. He did not dare tell Hamish how he had already called on Betty and reduced her to tears by saying he would tell Dick's boss that he, Dick, was consorting with a prostitute.

After the call was over, Hamish leaned back against the pillows with a sigh of satisfaction. His police station would soon be all his again.

Betty finally dried her eyes and surveyed the situation. Her daughter was due home at Christmas. That detective, Blair, would never leave her alone. What if her daughter found out? And poor Dick, who meant so much to her, would be ruined.

She sat down and began to write a letter to Dick. Her innocent time with him seemed to highlight the sordidness of her life. She had coped with it by being constantly on anti-depressants. Her daughter must never know how she had made her living. When the letter was finished, she went to get her supply of insulin. Betty, although she baked delicious cakes, hardly ever ate them because she was a diabetic. With a steady hand, she injected herself with a strong overdose, then went to lie down on her bed and close her eyes for the last time.

Dick set out that evening with a bunch of red roses and a diamond ring. How beautiful Sutherland looked on a starry night. His heart sang as he motored in a car rented from the local garage. His own car had not been found.

He parked in front of Betty's home, went up and rang the bell. There was no answer, and the house was in darkness. She had given him a key.

Dick unlocked the door and went in. The little hall was in darkness, but there was a light shining from under the living room door. "Betty!" he called and went into the living room. She wasn't there. He was about to turn away when he saw a letter addressed to himself in the middle of the coffee table.

She must have had to go out, he thought. He sat down on the couch, opened the envelope, and began to read.

"Dear Dick," he read. "It wouldn't have worked out. I couldn't bear the scandal. I couldn't bear it if my daughter found out. I never worked on her holidays. I want you to tear up this letter. I've made it look like an accident. There is no such thing as a tart with a heart. But the life coarsened me in a way that just recently has made me feel sick. But my precious girl must never know. I have taken an overdose of insulin.

"All my love,

"Betty."

Dick got slowly to his feet like an old man. He went into the bedroom and looked down at the dead figure of Betty on the bed.

He took out his phone and called Hamish.

Hamish found him sitting in the living room. Dick told him again what had happened and handed him the letter.

"You've got to get out o' here," said Hamish.

"I'm not ashamed of her."

"Nor should you be. But the two-faced Calvinists at police headquarters won't see it that way. You'll lose your job. Conduct unbecoming in a police officer and blah, blah, blah. You'll be dragged in for questioning. Your fingerprints must be all over the place. They may think you murdered her. Respect her last wishes and get out o' here. Come on. Let's dust the place, and get rid of that letter."

But Dick seemed incapable of moving. Hamish put on a pair of latex gloves and cleaned every surface he could think of. He took Betty's address book, looked up her daughter's college address in Cambridge, typed it out and printed it and left it on the desk. He found a travel bag and put the address book and computer into it, stuffing Dick's bouquet of roses along with them. He took Dick's car keys and drove his car to where he had parked the Land Rover some distance away.

When he returned, he urged Dick to his feet. "We'll go back in the Land Rover. You can collect the car another time. Come on, laddie. It's all over."

After giving Dick a couple of sleeping pills he had found in an old medicine chest, Hamish put him to bed and drove grimly to Strathbane. He had phoned Blair's wife, who was waiting for him in the bar of the Scotsman Hotel.

"What is it, Hamish?" she asked anxiously.

Hamish told her of the circumstances of Betty's death and her husband's threats.

"I'll kill the old bastard," said Mary passionately.

"Don't," said Hamish. "What I want to know is if you ever heard anything about Betty when you were on the game."

"Not a word. And we all pretty much knew what everyone else was up to. We didn't know about the foreign imports because that was before my time."

"For her daughter's sake, I want her to go to her grave as a respectable woman."

"I can do that."

"Now you're respectable and no one knows about you, could you claim her as a friend?"

"Least I can do."

"Good, here's the address. I left the door unlocked. Go and find the body and call the police and call her daughter.

I left her name and address on the desk. Betty went to the local kirk so the minister there will be glad to perform the funeral rites. Blair won't like it."

"Then he can get stuffed," said Mary. "It's as if he murdered her. Leave it to me."

"Tell me, Mary, could it have worked out?"

"I didn't know the woman. Look, my man is a drunken bastard but it suits me to be off the streets and have a nice home, and it's thanks to you I could change my identity. I can handle him because you never lose a sort of inner coarseness. I'm educated now and talk posh and look posh, but inside there's a tramp. Dick's a decent man. Give it a couple of years when romantic love fades and he might have begun to resent her past. I can't see any way it could have worked in the long run."

Hamish called in at police headquarters to see Jimmy and was told he had left. He ran him to earth in the pub. "Have the Campbell brothers started talking yet?" asked Hamish, sitting down next to him.

"Singing like canaries," said Jimmy. "It seems that Beryl was laundering money for them and acting as a courier, bringing money in from abroad. They swear it was Murdo himself who topped Gonzales and got them to clean up the mess in the cottage. Gonzales was trying to get more money for dealing drugs and was creaming off a lot of the profits. But we've got them for murdering Beryl and for the assault on you. Also, they claim they were told to dump Jessie's body in your garden, but they didn't kill her."

"And what about Cyril?"

"They said Cyril was an informant. But they swear blind they never touched him."

In the following weeks, Hamish was left with his bad conscience. If he hadn't manipulated Dick into meeting Betty, then none of this would have happened. Dick drifted around the police station like a ghost. He had lost weight. Dreary holidays came and went. They were spared any visits from Hetty because Hamish had told her that Dick had gone away to Glasgow to stay with relatives.

Sutherland seesawed its way through changes of climate. One week, the countryside was white under a raging blizzard and the following week, a false spring arrived with mild winds blowing in from the Gulf Stream.

Dick had a sudden impulse to visit Betty's grave. Hamish had gone out on his rounds to make sure people in the more remote crofts were all right. Dick had bought another old Ford.

He motored to the cemetery and began to wander through the graves, holding a vase and a bunch of white roses. At last he found the grave and crouched down and began to arrange the roses in the vase.

"Did you know my mother?" asked a voice behind him. Dick got to his feet and turned around. A lanky young woman with thick glasses stood looking at him.

"I was a friend," said Dick.

"I'm her daughter."

230 M. C. BEATON

"I'm very sorry for your loss," said Dick. "I thought you were at university."

"Half term. The minister told me that mother helped a lot of people. She often worked in the soup kitchen."

"She did indeed. A great lady."

"Mother wouldn't have wanted you to waste your money in flowers. Here!" She took out a wallet and extracted a twenty-pound note. "Buy yourself a meal."

"I do not need your money," said Dick, outraged. He stalked off.

When he got to the car, he sat trembling with outrage. Then he looked in the rearview mirror. His face was covered in grey stubble. He looked down at his clothes. He was wearing an old donkey jacket over a washed-out T-shirt. He realised his hair was straggling down the back of his neck. No wonder she had taken him for a down-and-out!

He drove into a barbershop in the town and got a shave and a haircut. He then bought new clothes: an anorak, wool sweater, and new trousers. He changed in the public toilet and left his old clothes behind.

When he got back to the police station, there was a note on the kitchen table. "Gone to Braikie. Shoplifting. Hamish."

Dick realised that he had been so sunk in gloom, he had barely noticed that Hamish had stopped taking him out on jobs.

He got back into his car and headed for Braikie. He

cruised around but couldn't see Hamish anywhere. He phoned him. "Nothing but a couple of schoolkids," said Hamish. "See you back at the station."

Dick was just driving past the library when he saw Shona leaving for her lunch. He stopped the car, got out, and followed her into the café.

"Why, Dick!" she exclaimed. "You're so thin!"

"Been having a hard time o' it," said Dick, sitting down opposite her.

"That makes two of us," said Shona, and began to cry.

"Here, lassie. Dinnae greet. Tell Dick all about it." He said to the waitress. "Leave us for a bit."

He handed Shona a handkerchief and waited until she had finished crying. "It's Diarmuid," she said. "He's broken off the engagement."

"Why?"

"He says I've been sleeping with half the men in Braikie."

"Oh, really? And what does dear Hetty have to say for herself?"

Shona looked at him in surprise. "What's Hetty got to do with it?"

"She's a spiteful, jealous cow. Where does this Diarmuid work?"

"In the town hall. In the sanitation department."

"It's Diarmuid Hendry, isn't it?"

"Yes, but…"

"Eat something. I'll be right back."

* * *

Dick went into the town hall and located the sanitation department. He flashed his warrant card and asked to speak to Mr. Hendry. He was ushered into a small cubicle of an office. Diarmuid rose to meet him. "What's this about, Officer?"

"Shona is very upset," said Dick. "I believe you've been listening to malicious lies from Hetty, her boss. There's not a word o' truth in any of it. I'm surprised you even listened to the woman."

Diarmuid looked awkward. "She was very convincing."

"Well, now you know it's all lies, you can get engaged again," said Dick.

Diarmuid sat down behind his desk and began to fiddle with a paper clip. Dick thought he looked like a geek with his oily black hair and thick glasses. He had expected Diarmuid to be handsome.

"There's a problem," said Diarmuid. "I've met someone else."

"You whit?" roared Dick.

"It just happened," mumbled Diarmuid. "I'm in love with her."

"You make me sick," raged Dick. "You cannae have loved Shona one bit, and I'll tell you this, she's had a lucky escape."

Dick went back to join Shona. "What did he say?" she asked.

"I'm afraid the turd has found someone else. Look,

Shona, pet, he's useless. If he'd really loved you, he wouldn't have believed Hetty for a moment. Maybe he didn't. Maybe he was already involved with this other lassie and wanted out. He's nothing but a streak o' piss. What did you see in him?"

"He was gentle. I had a boyfriend once who practically raped me. Diarmuid even said we could leave the sex bit until after we were married."

"Michty me!" Dick looked at her with shrewd eyes. "Does he live with his mother?"

"Yes, I met her. She was very sweet. She told me just how he likes his coffee in the morning and all his favourite food."

"Oh, she did, did she? Shona, look at me. The new lassie won't last long, either. Cheer up."

"I'll try."

"Want me to speak to Hetty?"

"Oh, no, please. It would be awful if you did. We've no proof. I'd better get back. Don't worry about me. I'll get over it."

Dick went back to Lochdubh and told Hamish all about Shona's aborted engagement.

Hamish looked at him blankly for a long time. Dick was just beginning to wonder if Hamish had heard a word he had said, when Hamish finally said, "I'll be damned. Here we've got an unbalanced woman. We've got one dead policeman, namely Cyril. It must have been

the biggest thing that ever happened to Hetty. Then he
dumped her. Do you think the crazy bitch might have
shot him?"

"It's more a man's murder," said Dick. "Has she even got
a shotgun?"

"If she has, I'll bet it isn't registered. For a moment, I was
thinking of seeing the provost and getting her fired. Then I
thought, she might kill Shona. The more I think of it, the
more I think we've had a murderer right under our noses all
this time."

"But how can we prove it?" asked Dick. "We don't have
enough to ask for a search warrant."

Hamish seized the Highlands and Islands phone book
and flipped through it. "Here we are. I'd forgotten the address. It's Number Four, The Loans. I'll get over there after
dark and scout around."

Hamish put on dark clothes that night and set out for
Braikie. He decided he'd better be careful. He had walked
into the Campbell brothers' trap like an idiot. He parked
the Land Rover several streets away.

Hetty, he remembered, lived in a tall old house, divided
into flats. Her apartment was on the ground floor. Thank
goodness for the Victorians and their love of shrubbery,
thought Hamish, easing himself into a thick clump of tall
bushes near the entrance.

He crouched down further as the light went on in Hetty's
flat. The door opened and a man came out. Hetty, wearing

a pink dressing gown, wrapped her arms around him and kissed him hungrily on the mouth.

"Good night," he said. "Don't forget Mother's invited us to tea tomorrow."

"I won't forget, Diarmuid. Nighty-night, darling."

Well, I'm blessed, thought Hamish. It's Shona's geek. He waited until Hetty had gone indoors again and Diarmuid had driven off and then wondered what to do. He could hardly break in while she was there.

Then he thought, she would be out for tea tomorrow. *Tea* would mean high tea, so probably around six o'clock. He decided to return the next day, stake out her house, and see if he could get in to make a search. He saw a lane up the side of the house and made his way there. There was a narrow road at the back. A gate led into Hetty's garden. It was shielded from the houses on either side by shrubbery and trees. That would be a good way to break in.

He returned to the station to tell Dick that Hetty was Diarmuid's latest love.

"What! Throw over Shona for that!" exclaimed Dick.

"I think sex is the answer. Maybe he was a virgin before she threw open her legs in welcome. I'll try to get into her flat."

Hamish went to the church the next morning. He wasn't religious but felt it his duty to attend and add another body to the congregation because he liked Mr. Wellington, the minister. The day was cold with thick mist. Mist had crept into the building and lay in bands across the interior of the church. The Currie sisters were there, screeching out the hymns in high falsettos while Mrs. Wellington boomed beside them.

The reading was from Romans about people being like the flowers of the field. The wind passes over them and then they are gone. How many deaths have I dealt with? thought Hamish. At least living in Lochdubh let him keep a mental balance. He knew most policemen working in cities could end up believing everyone was evil, and trusting no one.

When the service was over, he quickly left the church, nipping past the Currie sisters, who were debating the sermon with the minister as usual.

He returned to the police station, collected the dog and cat, and went for a walk along the waterfront. The mist seemed thicker than ever. He hoped it would last all day. The nights were getting lighter, but he knew it would be still dark by six o'clock.

"Don't get caught," urged Dick as Hamish set out. "If that one catches ye, she'll scream rape."

"I'll be careful," said Hamish.

He took Dick's car and drove to Braikie. Because the mist was still thick, he was only just able to see Diarmuid drive up and collect Hetty.

When they had gone off, he walked round to the road that led to the back of the villa. There were lights in the flats upstairs, but the flat next to Hetty's was in darkness. He climbed over the gate and went through the garden to the back door. It had only a simple Yale lock, which he sprang easily. Wearing latex gloves, he began his search.

He could not find anything incriminating. He even searched under the mattress in her bedroom. Then he heard the sound of a car arriving and stopping outside. He scuttled through to the kitchen and then stopped as he heard Hetty shouting, "What do you mean your mother doesn't like me?" And then came Diarmuid's voice. "Did you need to put so much make-up on? I think we should cool it, Hetty. I'll phone you."

"You dump me and look out!" screeched Hetty.

He heard the front door open and then slam. He crept out of the kitchen door, shutting it quietly behind him, and made his way down the garden. It was then that he saw a shed to the left of the gate. The light from the kitchen suddenly streamed down the garden. Hamish nipped over the gate and crouched down. He decided to wait until the coast was clear. He was suddenly determined to see what was in that shed.

He poked his head over the wall. Hetty was sitting at the kitchen table, a glass in her hand.

The evening dragged on. The cold mist seemed to be creeping into Hamish's very bones. He suddenly flattened himself lower to the ground when he heard the kitchen door open. He heard Hetty come down the garden. He heard the click of a key and the rattle of a chain. She was opening the shed.

He risked a look over the garden wall. She was carrying a large bag. Hetty went into the kitchen and closed the curtains.

What was in the bag? More booze?

Or what if, thought Hamish, his mind making a sudden leap, it contained a shotgun. If Hetty rejected by Cyril had shot him, maybe she planned to do the same to Diarmuid.

He sprinted to his car and drove nearer to her villa with the lights off and waited.

After ten minutes she appeared, carrying the bag. She put it in the boot of her car, got in, and drove off. Hamish let her get a bit ahead and began to follow. But after several turnings, he lost her.

Suddenly afraid, he went straight to Shona's flat. She would know where Diarmuid lived.

Diarmuid and his mother, Abigail Hendry, were drinking cocoa in front of the television.

"I'm sorry, Mother," said Diarmuid. "I didn't know she was such a harridan."

She was a small woman, neatly dressed with short grey hair in the helmet fashion so beloved of Braikie hairdressers. "Quiet, now, darling. I do so love David Attenborough. Look at the funny penguin."

There came a hammering at the door. "Who can that be?" wondered Diarmuid.

"Don't answer!" said his mother sharply. "Someone should have had the decency to phone."

There then came the sound of breaking glass. Diarmuid ran into the hall in time to see a hand stretch inside the door and unlock it. He stood there, paralysed with fright, as Hetty entered wearing a long cloak.

"Hetty, I'm calling the police," he babbled.

"What is it, dear?" called his mother.

Hetty thrust Diarmuid aside, went into the living room, took out a sawn-off shotgun from under her cloak, and shot Mrs. Hendry full in the chest.

She reloaded and went back into the hall. Diarmuid had fainted. He was slumped against the wall. He had peed himself, and his trousers were wet.

"Now, you," said Hetty. "But I want you awake to see this." There was a vase of flowers on the hall table. She tipped the contents, water, flowers, and all, over him.

He opened his eyes and screamed with fear.

"Think you can dump me," said Hetty, raising the gun.

Hamish Macbeth hurtled through the open door and crashed his full weight right into Hetty, sending her flying. The gun went skittering across the tiles of the hall. He jumped on top of her, flipped her over, and handcuffed her while she let out a stream of swear words.

When she fell silent, he took out his phone and called Strathbane. "You can just see the tiger closing in on his prey," said David Attenborough's voice from the television in the living room.

Hamish looked into the living room and shuddered.

* * *

When Hetty was taken off to Strathbane, Hamish sat in Jimmy's car, feeling sick.

"What put you on to her?" said Jimmy.

"I thought she might have something to do with the death of Cyril. She was getting madder and madder." Hamish decided to say nothing about having broken into her house. It would mean he would be suspended from duty and possibly sacked. "I arrived when Diarmuid was telling her it was all off. I was heading back to Lochdubh when it suddenly dawned on me that if she had shot Cyril because of rejection, she just might do the same to Diarmuid. I got Diarmuid's address from Shona. It's a wonder Hetty didn't crow over Shona. Maybe she wanted to wait until she got a ring on her finger."

"Where's Blair?"

"Off duty."

"Right," said Jimmy. "Let's leave the forensic boys and the pathologist to do their work and get back to Strathbane. I suppose you want to be in on the interview."

"I want to see if she confesses to murdering Cyril," said Hamish.

Hetty looked at them with dull eyes when they entered the interview room. A policewoman set up the recording and video equipment, Jimmy went through the formalities, and the questioning began.

"Why did you kill Mrs. Hendry?" he asked.

"Diarmuid would have married me if she hadn't got in the way," said Hetty.

"Where did you get the shotgun?"

"Can you bring me my make-up and a change of clothes?" asked Hetty.

"I'm sure that can be arranged," said Jimmy.

"I'll be in all the newspapers and on television," said Hetty.

"So you will," said Hamish in a soft voice. "Of course, if you confessed to killing Cyril Sessions, you would be *world-famous*."

Her eyes glittered. "Really?"

"Oh, yes."

She banged both hands on the table, making them jump. "Well, I did!" she said triumphantly.

"We'll start with the murder of Cyril Sessions. Tell us about that."

"He made love to me. He said we would go away together. He made me do things in the bedroom no man should ask a decent woman to do." She smiled. "Anal sex can be very painful, and all that near-strangulation business."

Poor Betty, thought Hamish. Cyril must have made her feel really dirty.

"But then he kept asking and asking about Macbeth. I lost my rag and said I thought he fancied Macbeth, and he said he was on an assignment to spy on him."

"Why didn't you tell us this?" asked Hamish.

"Forgot," said Hetty. "Anyway, when he stopped seeing me or answering my calls and I thought of all the dirty things he'd made me do, I decided the world would be better off without him. I got my gun…"

"Where did you get the gun?" asked Jimmy.

"It was my father's. I found it when he died and kept it."

"What was your father doing with a sawn-off shotgun?"

"He robbed shops and things," she said airily.

"Name?"

"Gary McCue."

"That's not your name."

"He forgot to marry my mother. I've always used her name."

Jimmy took a deep breath. "So you decided to murder Cyril?"

"I stole a motorbike. I had it all planned. I'm very clever. I went down to Glasgow and bought the helmet and leathers in case you started checking the shops around here. I waited up on the moors where I could see down into Lochdubh. I followed him to that beach and blasted him."

"But you must have seen me leave and have known he was following me," said Hamish. "Weren't you worried I might catch you?"

"I drove across the moors and saw you go on ahead and Cyril go down to that beach. Easy."

The questioning went on until Jimmy decided to take a break.

* * *

Hamish and Jimmy went to the pub. "Think she's sane?" asked Jimmy.

"Sane enough to go to trial," said Hamish. "I don't know if I'll ever forgive myself. I was so focussed on Murdo or one of his gang being the murderer that I thought she was batty but harmless."

"I need a stiff drink before we go back in there."

Blair arrived at headquarters, tipped off about the arrest. Hearing that Jimmy was taking a break from the questioning and determined to seize the glory, he collected Detective Andy McNab and decided to interview Hetty himself.

He roared, he shouted, he fired question after question at her. Hetty began to shake and tremble, no longer sustained with dreams of being a killer celebrity.

The room began to swim around her. She fainted, fell forward, banged her head on the corner of the table, and fell unconscious to the floor.

Blair rushed to get the medical officer. Hamish and Jimmy came back to find chaos and Blair wailing to Daviot that it was an accident. Hetty was rushed to hospital, where she was diagnosed with a severe concussion.

Daviot demanded the recording of the interview. He watched it uneasily. If Hetty got a lawyer, it was possible the police would be blamed for bullying and harassment. He called Blair into his office and said severely, "This is a bad business. It was Macbeth who stopped it turning into two murders. You should have left Anderson and Macbeth to get on with the questioning."

"I know, sir," said Blair, all false meekness. "But Macbeth and Anderson had taken off to the pub—and in the middle of an important interview. Very unprofessional. I am right sorry, sir, but I was doing what I thought was my duty, sir."

"Very well. I will talk to you later. Send Macbeth and Anderson in."

When Hamish and Jimmy walked in, Daviot looked at them coldly. Hamish was not wearing his uniform, and Jimmy was smelling strongly of whisky.

"If you had both not decided drinking was more important than interviewing a murderer, Mr. Blair would never have had to take over. I am very displeased."

"We didnae cause the lassie to faint and knock herself out," said Jimmy.

"I do not think Mr. Blair did, either," said Daviot. Blair always showed him respect and called him sir, unlike these two mavericks. "Why are you out of uniform, Macbeth?" he asked.

"I just happened to be in Braikie and I was going to have another word with her when I heard her boyfriend dumping her. I suddenly wondered if she had killed Cyril after he rejected her and decided to wait and see what she would do. I followed her when she left but it was thick mist. I found Diarmuid's address and went there in time to stop her killing Diarmuid Hendry."

"It's a pity you didn't consider her a suspect earlier," said Daviot.

"If it hadnae been for Hamish, we'd never have got her," said Jimmy.

"Go and write up your reports," said Daviot.

After they had gone, Daviot reflected that he hated the way Hamish Macbeth always made him look like a fool. Blair could be awkward but he was always respectful, never forgot Mrs. Daviot's birthday, and was a good member of the lodge. Somehow, life would be more comfortable without Hamish Macbeth constantly showing up the shortcomings of headquarters. He did not like the fact that Hamish had seen those awful photographs of his wife.

Daviot knew there was a push to sell off police stations. If the police station in Lochdubh was sold off, he was sure Hamish would never accept a transfer to Strathbane. He would leave the police force. He began to make plans.

Hamish returned to the police station after a long night. He had typed his report and then called at the hospital to find that Hetty had suffered bleeding from the brain and was undergoing an operation.

As he got ready for bed, he could hear snores coming from Dick's bedroom. He reflected sadly that his guilt over introducing Dick to Betty would now stop him from trying to get rid of the man.

He slept for six hours and then rose and dressed and

went into the living room. Dick hurriedly switched off the television.

"Anything on the news?" asked Hamish.

"Just a bit."

"Put it on. It's coming up to the top of the hour."

"Wouldn't you like some breakfast first?"

"Just switch the damn thing on."

Dick did as he was bid. On Grampian TV, the arrest of Hetty was the first item, and there was Blair flanked by Daviot outside police headquarters.

"Thanks to our expert detective work," said Daviot, "we have arrested Hetty Dunstable for the murders of Cyril Sessions and Mrs. Abigail Hendry." Blair smirked modestly at the cameras. "I am not taking any questions at the moment. A full press release will be given to you later."

"You know," said Hamish bitterly, "I wouldnae mind a bit o' credit, just the once. You know what's up with a lot of police force today, Dick? Promotion is given to the ones who crawl to the hierarchy."

"But you never want promotion," said Dick.

"No, but a thank-you wouldn't go amiss. I'm going out for a walk."

It was a clear, cold day. The water of the loch lay as calm as a mirror. A car drove up and stopped behind him. Elspeth got out.

"Sent back up here," she said. "I've been to Braikie to talk to the neighbours and by all reports you were the one on the scene and yet Daviot never mentioned you. I've sent off a report and film of what the neighbours say."

"Daviot'll never forgive me," said Hamish.

"It goes out on the six o'clock news."

"I'll be swamped wi' the press. I'll need to go off and hide. Couldn't you have left me out of it?"

"No. Too good a story. What's the latest on the mad librarian?"

"The operation was successful. She tried to say that Blair had struck her, until she was told they had the whole thing on tape."

"If I bring the crew down, Hamish, can I do an interview?"

"No."

"You know, Hamish, I've helped you a lot in the past. I think the least you could do is to help me."

"I don't like emotional blackmail," said Hamish, unconsciously echoing Priscilla, and strode off along the waterfront with his pets scampering at his heels.

Epilogue

I waive the quantum o' the sin,
The hazard of concealing;
But och! It hardens a' within,
And petrifies the feeling!

—*Robert Burns*

Winter finally loosened its grip on the Highlands. A blustery mild wind bent the daffodils in the Currie sisters' garden and sent little white choppy waves scurrying across the surface of the loch. The snow retreated up to the tops of the mountains. Fresh green leaves appeared on the rowan trees.

Hamish Macbeth went about his usual duties; a shoplifting case here, a burglary there, and checking sheep dip papers.

The following month he was due to appear in the High Court in Edinburgh as a witness for the prosecution in

Hetty's trial. He reflected sourly that Blair and Daviot would no longer be able to cover up his part in the investigation. Elspeth's interviews with the neighbours had not appeared. He always wondered if she had got it scrapped and then thought ruefully that it was all he deserved for having been so rude to her.

He was just checking on his sheep one morning when his mobile phone rang. It was Jimmy. "Hetty's topped herself," he said.

"How?" asked Hamish.

"Tore strips off her sheets and hanged herself from the bars. Save you a trip to Edinburgh."

"So it will go down in history that Strathbane solved the case," said Hamish.

"It's your own fault for being so unambitious," said Jimmy heartlessly.

"Did she ever say what she did with that motorbike?"

"Aye, she pushed it over the cliffs up the coast. It's somewhere at the bottom o' the Minch. See you."

Well, that was that, thought Hamish.

Dick decided to go and call on Shona. Not that he was interested in her any more, he thought. But somehow the spring weather tugged at his emotions, waking old feelings.

He patted his brand-new scarlet Ford Fiesta before getting into it. He had appeared on a quiz programme on Grampian TV called *Gimme the Answer* and the new car had been the result. Grampian TV was the one station where he had not been blacklisted.

He carefully timed his arrival to coincide with Shona's lunch hour. He stood beside his car and waited for her to come down the library steps.

Dick's heart beat quickly when she appeared. "Hi, Shona," he said. "Fancy a bit of lunch?"

"That'd be grand. I'm head librarian now."

They walked into the café and ordered their food.

The sunlight shone through the café window and sent little fiery sparks shining from an engagement ring on Shona's finger.

Dick experienced a little pang of disappointment. He pointed to the ring. "Who's the lucky fellow?"

"It's Diarmuid."

"Whit!" Dick turned red with outrage. "That stupid, useless..."

She put a hand over his. "Be happy for me. He's a good man."

"How can a good man even think about getting his leg over such as Hetty?"

"But he didn't! He said she chased him."

"Shona, please consider..."

"No," she said mulishly, "I thought you would be happy for me."

"I don't feel like eating," said Dick, and marched out of the café.

* * *

Hamish listened sympathetically to Dick as he ranted and raved on his return to the police station.

When Dick had finally fallen silent, Hamish said, "Have you ever considered that the lovely Shona may not be that bright?"

"She's a librarian," said Dick.

"I didn't mean intellectually bright. She's a small-town girl. She's getting on for thirty. A chap in the council with his own home will be considered quite a catch in Braikie."

"What a waste," muttered Dick.

"I'm taking a few days off," said Hamish suddenly.

"Is that all right with headquarters?"

"Cover for me."

"Okay. Why don't you and me take a holiday together?"

Just like Darby and Joan, thought Hamish gloomily. "It wouldn't work," he said. "They'd never let us go off together."

"So where are you going?"

"Just a trip."

"Where?"

"Mind your own business."

The following morning, Dick looked suspiciously at Hamish as he set out, wearing his best suit and with his fiery hair brushed till it shone.

He's going to see Elspeth, he thought. That's all I need.

Hamish drove to Inverness airport and caught a plane to Glasgow. He then took a taxi to the television station where

Elspeth worked. He was told that one of the staff was leaving and they had all gone for a celebratory lunch to Rogano's restaurant. Hamish thought of his small bank balance. Rogano's was an upmarket fish restaurant, and he wouldn't have a chance to talk to Elspeth alone anyway. He told the receptionist he would wait.

He collected a cup of black coffee from the coffee machine. It was scalding hot. He took a small cardboard container from the watercooler and looked around for somewhere to pour off a bit of the coffee before adding cold water. His eye lit on three wineglasses and a bunch of grapes on a small white table. All the glasses of wine, white, red, and yellow, were half empty. He tipped some of his coffee into the red wine.

The receptionist shrieked. "You can't do that! That's an art exhibit. It's called *After Dinner* and cost a fortune."

"Sorry," said Hamish miserably. "But if you tip out the red wine and half fill the glass no one will know."

She scurried off and returned with a thin man with dangling earphones who was carrying a bottle of red wine and a jug and proceeded to repair the damage.

The day dragged on while Hamish tried to read magazines, looking up hopefully every time someone came through the doors.

At last Elspeth arrived with a crowd of people. She stopped short at the sight of Hamish. "What are you doing here?"

"I came to see you."

"Why?"

"Just to see you," said Hamish, suddenly wishing he had not come. She looked very sophisticated and not like the Elspeth of the Highlands.

"I've got to get to work. Look, if you can wait until after the six o'clock news, we'll go out for a quick drink."

She marched off towards the lifts.

Hamish gloomily looked at the magazines. They seemed to be full of features on celebrities he had never heard of. Suddenly he fell into a deep sleep, and he dreamt that Hetty was chasing him across the moors with a shotgun.

He woke to find Elspeth shaking him. "Let's go," she said. "I haven't much time."

They walked to a pub nearby.

"So what do you want to talk about?" asked Elspeth.

"I came to apologise. I felt I was rude to you the last time we met."

Her face softened. "And you came all this way! You should have warned me."

"I came on an impulse. Look, Elspeth, is there any hope for us?"

Her silver eyes surveyed him. "I wouldn't want to leave my job here," she said. "Would you want to leave Lochdubh and work for Strathclyde police?"

"No."

"So you see, it's hardly a case of the world well lost for love. I don't want to go back there. You don't want to come here. There's your answer."

"You could always give up work."

"And live on a policeman's salary? I've got used to all the comforts that money can bring, Hamish."

"So there's nothing more to be said?"

"No, let's drop it. Tell me how things are in Lochdubh."

They chatted away until Elspeth looked at her watch. "I've got to get back."

"Can you put me up for the night?" asked Hamish.

"Sorry. Bad idea."

Well, I tried, thought Hamish as he parked the Land Rover outside the police station. Dick looked anxiously as he walked in and then visibly brightened. "Would you like something to eat?"

"No," said Hamish. "I just want to go to bed."

"There's an official-looking letter arrived for you."

"Let's see it."

Hamish opened the letter and stared down at the contents in dismay. It was to tell him that the police station in Lochdubh was to be closed down. It would be sold off in six months' time. Hamish dumbly handed the letter to Dick.

"They cannae dae that!" said Dick, looking wildly around.

"I'll think o' something," said Hamish grimly.

In the morning, Hamish brushed and pressed his uniform trousers and removed several hen feathers from his regulation sweater. One of the epaulettes looked about to come loose, so he stitched it firmly on. Then he polished his boots until they shone.

"Where are you going?" asked Dick.

"To fight," said Hamish. "Sonsie, Lugs, come along."

He reflected as he walked out to the Land Rover that it should not be such a perfect day. Lochdubh dreamt in golden sunlight. Groups of villagers were standing outside Patel's shop gossiping.

He put his pets in the back and drove off. As he passed the Tommel Castle Hotel, he saw Priscilla crossing the car park. He was about to stop, but decided to drive on. I've had enough o' rejection, he thought, and thon one is a walking example.

Never would he work in Strathbane. He cursed Blair and Daviot and every creeping sneak that had ever plagued his career. Policing was about helping people, bringing justice, not meeting stupid government targets and crawling like mad in a scramble for promotion. Okay, people thought it was weird that he was not ambitious. But maybe Scotland could do with a few more unambitious policemen.

He went in to headquarters. As he passed the detectives' room, Jimmy hailed him and came hurrying out. "I just heard the news, Hamish. Is there anything I can do?"

"You can't. I can. Let me past."

Jimmy stared after Hamish as he walked up the stairs. Blair's jeering voice came from behind Jimmy. "Aye, there he goes. Off tae the scaffold."

* * *

"You can't go in there. He's busy. I won't allow it," said Helen, trying to bar the way.

Hamish put her bodily to one side, opened the door, and marched in.

Daviot rose from behind his desk. "You can't come in here without an appointment," he said.

Hamish slammed a folder down on the desk.

"Have a look at that!"

Daviot opened the folder and turned a muddy colour as he found himself looking down at one of those dreadful photographs of his wife.

"You told me you'd destroyed these," he cried.

"Keeping one is a dirty trick," said Hamish, "but so is closing down my police station. I saved your job, *sir*. So look at it this way. No police station for me means no job for you. Did this order come from above? I can find out."

"I was ordered to cut costs, and the policing could be done from here. We could give you a promotion."

"I hate doing this," said Hamish, "but if I must, I must. Give me back my station or this goes out to the newspapers."

"I can be a dangerous enemy," said Daviot.

"And I can be worse," said Hamish.

Daviot put his head in his hands. Then he mumbled, "Your bloody police station is safe."

Hamish picked up the folder.

"Leave that here!" shouted Daviot.

"Insurance," said Hamish, and walked out.

He ought to feel triumphant, he thought as he climbed into the Land Rover. But he felt dirty. It's as if I've become one of them, he thought.

He stopped up on the moors, well clear of Strathbane, and let the dog and cat out to chase each other through the heather. He stood beside the Land Rover, took off his cap, and threw it on the passenger seat. A jaunty little wind ruffled his red hair. Far up in the clear blue sky, a pair of mating buzzards dipped and turned.

"The hell wi' all of them," he said aloud. "It's worth it."

"Talking to yourself, laddie?"

Hamish swung round. The gnarled figure of an old crofter, Robbie Sinclair, appeared round the Land Rover.

"Why is it," demanded Hamish, "that when I want a witness to a crime, no one's seen anything, but when I have a wee chat with myself someone like you always creeps up out the heather?"

"Your sins will find you out," said Robbie sententiously.

"Talking to myself isn't a sin. Why am I even bothering to explain?" said Hamish. "What are you doing around here?"

"I was out for a dauner," said Robbie, "and I saw the police vehicle. Got a ciggie?"

"No, I gave up smoking."

"So did I," said Robbie, "but I aye crave just the one. Well, I'd better get on. Some of us have work tae do."

"Like what?" asked Hamish, but Robbie was already scuttling away across the moor.

Hamish went into the kitchen. Dick looked up with tears in his eyes. "I was just taking a look around, Hamish, and it's breaking my heart."

"Then you can mend your heart," said Hamish. "I've saved the station."

Dick rose, rushed round the table, and hugged Hamish. "Get off me, you daft bugger," said Hamish, pushing him away.

"This calls for a drink," said Dick. "I'll switch the telly on now."

"Why? What's happened?"

"Angela's on the book show on the telly."

"Right! Let's have a look."

Dick switched on the television and went to the cupboard where he kept all his goodies.

He brought down a bottle of Armagnac, then went through to the kitchen and came back with two glasses. "I've been saving this for a special occasion." He poured two glasses and handed one to Hamish. "Slainte!"

"Slainte," echoed Hamish.

The book show opened to two presenters, a man and a woman, sitting on a sofa. Both were dressed identically in tartan shirts and jeans.

"Our first guest," said the man, "is T. J. Leverage, whose detective story *A Very Highland Murder* is climbing up the charts. Come and join us, T. J."

Angela appeared dressed in the full evening outfit she had worn for the sofa awards.

The woman presenter laughed. "Do you always wear full evening dress in the middle of the day, T. J.?"

"From time to time," said Angela calmly. "I find standards of dress have slipped badly. Men and women seem to dress alike these days."

"That's my girl," laughed Hamish. "She's got herself a new backbone. I love that woman!"

"She's married," said Dick sharply.

"Oh, drink your drink and shut up," said Hamish, feeling trapped again. He did not hear the rest of the interview because he became lost in a Walter Mitty dream where someone had taken lewd photographs of Dick and he, Hamish, was saying, "Leave my police station or these photos go to the press."

As he walked along the waterfront later, he had a superstitious feeling that the old capricious gods of Sutherland were going to make him pay for his bad behaviour. He had involved Dick with a prostitute who had subsequently taken her life. He had just blackmailed his boss.

As he reached the doctor's house, a cab drove up and Angela, still in full evening dress, got out.

"Did you see the show, Hamish?"

"Aye, all of it," lied Hamish, who felt he could hardly tell her he had missed practically all of it, fantasising about blackmailing Dick out of the police station. "See you put the lot on."

"I had to," said Angela, paying off the cabbie. "It was hanging in my closet, accusing me of extravagance. I'd help that lassie with her rucksack if I were you."

Outside Mrs. Mackenzie's, a slight young woman was bent under the weight of a heavy rucksack.

Hamish walked up to her. "Help you with that?"

"Please. I've been walking and I am so fatigued."

She had a French accent. Hamish helped her lift the rucksack from her shoulders. "Visiting?" he asked.

"Yes, I am tired of sleeping in the outdoors and someone told me that I could rent a room here."

"Are you French?"

"Yes, from Lyons. But my mother was English."

She smiled up at him. She had a little triangular face and big brown eyes. From her sensible walking gear drifted the aroma of some French perfume.

"All I need," she said, "is a drink and a meal that I don't have to cook."

"Why don't I help you in," said Hamish. "I'll take you for a meal. I am Police Sergeant Hamish Macbeth."

She dimpled up at him. Her eyelashes were very thick and long. "And I am Michelle Dulange. Is this a part of the local police service?"

"Oh, definitely," said Hamish happily.

He helped her in and then waited outside.

Hamish was just beginning to think she had forgotten him when after twenty minutes she appeared wearing a white sweater over a short skirt and high heels.

In the Italian restaurant, waiter Willie Lamont ushered them to the table at the window. "A friend o' Hamish's?" asked Willie.

"I am a French tourist, and this policeman is kindly taking me for lunch."

"The amount o' French letters I've had," said Willie, leaning against the table.

"We don't want to know about your sex life, Willie," said Hamish sharply.

Willie looked surprised. "Nothing to do with sex. I had a pen pal in Dijon when I was at school. I mind…"

"Go away and bring the menus," ordered Hamish.

They ordered avocado and prawns followed by escalope Marsala. Hamish poured out wine and smiled at his pretty companion. "Tell me about yourself," said Hamish.

She looked towards the window. "Who is that lady?"

Hamish followed her gaze. Priscilla stood outside, looking at them. He gave her a long, flat stare, trying to signal, don't dare come in here. Priscilla walked on.

During the next few days, Hamish neglected his duties and took Michelle for long drives around the countryside. On her last night, Dick made them dinner. He noticed that Michelle showed no signs of leaving. He collected the dog and cat, drove up to the Tommel Castle Hotel, and begged a cheap room for the night.

In the morning, Hamish turned over in bed but Michelle was gone. It had been a night to remember. He quickly washed and dressed and hurried along to Mrs. Mackenzie's. To his amazement, he learned that Michelle had left. He rushed back, got into the Land Rover, and drove out of Lochdubh. Just beyond the Tommel Castle Hotel, he saw her small figure under the large rucksack walking along the road. He parked and jumped out. "Michelle! Why did you leave just like that?"

"It was fun, wasn't it?" she said. "Such a good time. But now I must keep to my schedule."

"Marry me!" said Hamish desperately.

"Oh, my dear Hamish. I do love you."

"Then marry me."

"How can I say it? What is it people say? It's a nice place to visit but I wouldn't want to stay there. Besides, I have a *cher ami* waiting for me in Lyon. A good catch. His family has vineyards. Au revoir."

Hamish miserably watched her go. He drove back to Lochdubh, got down from the Land Rover, and leaned on the wall overlooking the loch.

"Grand day," said Archie Maclean, joining him.

"Do you understand women, Archie?"

"Never have, never will. Where's your French friend?"

"Gone off on her travels."

"Aye, weel, some o' the lassies are like that. They've become chust like us fellows. Easy come, easy go. Better get hame afore the wife comes looking for me."

Hamish watched him walk away. He suddenly found that he was not suffering. The episode with Michelle seemed to be fading fast.

He looked around at the village of Lochdubh and at his police station.

He laughed. "My kingdom," he said. "I wouldnae change it for the world."